THE PARKOUR CLUB

PAM WITHERS

AROOJ HAYAT

Pam Withers, Author

Arooj Hayat, Author

The Parkour Club

Published in Canada by Pam Withers and Arooj Hayat, www.
pamwithers.com

Issues in print and electronic formats.
ISBN 978-0-9959103-2-4 (paperback)
ISBN 978-0-9959103-3-1 (epub)

Cover design: Jonas Perez
Interior design: Stephanie Candiago

Arooj Hayat: I dedicate this book to you, the young Muslims, who know the struggle of living as a "visible Muslim" in this society. I know how hard it is growing up with your feet in two worlds, striving to strike a balance, and always having to act like an ambassador for your religion and your culture. And yet, you all keep doing good, smiling, and winning at whatever you choose to take on. Keep it up!

I also wish to dedicate this book to my little daughter, my nieces and nephews, and ALL the children of their generation, growing up in a scary world. May Allah always protect you, strengthen you with moral clarity, conviction, faith, and patience, and make you a shining beacon of hope for a better future, Ameen.

THE PARKOUR CLUB

Parkour involves moving from one point to another as quickly and efficiently as possible. Parkour athletes are known as traceurs and traceuses. Having originated in France, the sport has spread worldwide. Freerunning, sometimes used interchangeably with parkour, includes tricking moves such as aerial rotations and spins, which go beyond parkour.

———

"If you want to make peace, you don't talk to your friends. You talk to your enemies." — Moshe Dayan, Israeli military leader, politician and crusader for peace (Newsweek, October 17, 1977)

———

"When did we start to scare so easily? Why don't we assume goodwill in one another? Why do we not ask questions of each other, learn from one another?" — Elamin Abdelmahmoud, CBC Opinion, February 28, 2017 (also social media editor, BuzzFeed Canada)

CHAPTER ONE

I LIE IN BED WITH A TEAR-SOAKED PILLOW UNDER ME, another pressed down on my head, trying to drown out the stream of words coming from my parents' bedroom.

"...left because it was too dangerous!"

"...one little incident and your paranoia..."

"...to keep Bronte safe!"

"...don't blame this on Bronte..."

"...you ever coming home?"

"Shhh, she'll hear..."

I pull the pillow down harder on my head. Now just muffled crying reaches my ears. Great. Families that cry together, die together. No, girl! Bad rhyme! Okay, families that weep together, keep together? Lame, Bronte. Concentrate. Get the right rhyme, and it'll all work out. I'm kinda superstitious about rhymes. They also help me chill when I'm stressed.

"Be strong to be useful," I tell myself. It's the international parkour motto: *Etre fort pour être utile.*

But that, too, fails to rally me like it usually does, 'cause I can't undo what Mom has done. It's her fault we're coming apart, which means it'll be her fault if Dad gets killed.

Dad's famous, an American TV war correspondent. Covers all the Middle East. How exciting and important is that?! A year ago, the three of us moved to relatively safe Alexandria, Egypt, a city of five million. That allowed Dad to come home between assignments to the comfort of family, and me to attend school there whenever I wasn't working out at the glass-domed Alexandria Parkour Academy. I *loved* living in Egypt!

Then came one little terrorist bombing in our neighbourhood – no one even died – and Mom totally freaked out. She acted like we were suddenly in a war zone or at the start of World War III or something. I mean, sure it was scary. For one whole minute. But seriously not worth turning our family upside-down for! I was hiding behind the white sofa in the den eavesdropping when they had their big fight.

"Enough!" my mom screams at my dad, shaking the newspaper at him. "Could've been us! We're probably targets, being white! I'm not living here another minute!"

"Karen, darling, you're over-reacting. It was an unfortunate one-off. This is one of the safest neighbourhoods in one of the safest cities in the Middle East," Dad points out.

Way safer than all the places Dad goes, duh, I think.

"How can you say that, Frank?" she shouts in her drama-queen voice. "We could've been hit! Bronte could've died! You'd sacrifice your own wife and daughter for this crazy new job of yours?" She's flapping her hands like she's fighting off an invasion of masked terrorists with her favorite pink dish towel, high heels stomping dents into the living room's thick Arabian carpet.

"Honey, be reasonable. This was a big promotion, a plum

job for me. You were excited when I first got it. You know it pays our rent and vacations and your club memberships and Bronte's parkour lessons. We agreed to move here and it has been working out just fine. Bronte loves it."

"Bronte doesn't know anything! She's sixteen! And she's way too lippy since we got here!"

"Karen, she's a normal teenager. A bright, happy one at that."

"Maybe around you, not around me. And don't tell me to be reasonable when there are bombs going off practically next door. I've had it, Frank. Don't you see? I'll have a nervous breakdown if I have to live in this country one day longer. I'm sorry to leave you to your workaholic, dangerous lifestyle, which *you chose*, but I'm going home, and taking Bronte with me. You can't stop me. Join us there or not, as you please."

I feel myself go cold and shudder all over as I press my face into the wall.

"Have you even asked Bronte?" Dad asks, sounding more resigned by the minute. Resigned, desperate, defeated? No way this all started with the one random bomb explosion, I reflect, pain forming at the back of my throat. Seems to me Mom started attacking Dad (and me) unfairly for anything and everything a few months after the overseas move. She's a coward, a douchebag, not cut out to be a war correspondent's wife. Or my mother?

I push my sweaty face out from behind the sofa.

"Shhh, Karen." Dad tries to hug her. As she pushes him away, Dad's hands go limp and his chin lowers to his chest. That's when I flee, tears staining the hardwood steps and hallway all the way to my bedroom, hands over my ears.

So Dad returned to the USA with us last week, quiet and

hunched most of the way, me all but clinging to him. Now he's headed back to the Middle East without us. Temporarily or permanently? Is it because of his work, or is his work just an excuse to flee his fizzling marriage? I'll start waterworks again if I linger on those questions.

As I punch my wet pillow, the sound of my parents' door opening makes me pull myself together.

"Dad!" I shout, leaping up and rushing out to bury myself in his arms. Mom appears at the bedroom door, her face gray and set, body turned away. He holds me tight, our heads touching. "Don't go, Dad!"

"I have to, Bronte," he says gently. "I'm off to Yemen to cover a ceasefire."

"As if those ever hold. As if anyone should ever go to Yemen!" I plead. It's the poorest, most dysfunctional country in the Middle East. As dysfunctional as our family. All I want is for us to be happy and together, like we were a year ago.

"I'll call and write," he promises, his voice cracking. "I love you, Bronte."

Lips plant a kiss on the top of my head, on the yellow hair that's the same color as his. Then he's down the stairs, out the front door, and in a taxi—without having promised he'll be back.

CHAPTER TWO

For an hour after Dad's taxi leaves, I cry the equivalent volume of Alexandria's saltwater bay. Bedroom door locked, dresser shoved against it, I totally ignore Mom's knocking and her quiet offers of a warm supper. I consider climbing out the window and running away, but Mom has my passport and I have no experience as a bank robber, which is what I'd have to be in order to buy a ticket back to Egypt.

So I sigh and gaze out the window at the lights flickering on in our desert town. Am I really back here in boring Rich-land, Washington, USA, population less than 50,000?

Feels like a million years since I was a sophomore here. I prefer Alexandria: the slick, cultivated seaport of the Mediterranean. I prefer hummus to hamburgers, baklava to banana bread, Turkish coffee to Taster's Choice Instant. High heels to sneakers, except when I'm doing parkour. America has no idea how it sucks in the cuisine department, fashion department (especially shoes) and, at least at Three Rivers High School, the babe department.

Yeah, that's the real reason I wanted to stay in Egypt. Sarfraz. Dreamy brown eyes, perfect bod, gentle and mysterious. Too mysterious the final weeks, but that's another story. My secret boyfriend.

I toss my pillows off the bed and grab my tablet.

"Sarfraz, I miss u. Ask me 2 come back & I will. ILU. Bronte"

Of course, I delete everything, letter by letter, tears plopping on the screen in the process.

To banish terrifying thoughts of Dad getting shot in some messed-up civil war, I let my mind drift back my last Parkour Academy visit in Alexandria.

"How's my American star?" the instructor greets me in his shaky English with his ever-amped-up smile as I step into the facility. "Come to wow us with one of your high-velocity sessions?"

"That's the plan." I smile, but my eyes are darting around the gym, from the toddlers jumping and hanging in the kiddies' corner, to the sea of colourful gym mats and wooden constructions that make this gigantic, brightly lit facility the city's coolest indoor playground.

A dozen guys are bounding about, leaping from handhold to foothold, rolling, flipping, swarming the obstacles. In one corner, girls a few years younger than me, the ones I help lotsa times, wear loose cotton pants, sweatshirts, and hijabs, which cover their hair and neck. The headgear dangles from all angles as their bare feet run up walls, launch their little bodies into the air, and land ninja-like on the mats to a mosh-pit of giggles. Their sparkly orange toenail polish, in cool contrast to their dark clothing, makes me grin.

"Nice going!" I say, offering a thumbs-up, but again my eyes are skimming the room, looking for *him*.

From a far corner, a long, lithe body in black vest and sweatpants hurls itself into space, all but brushing the glass-domed ceiling twenty feet over our heads. As if on invisible aerial-artist wires, his body twists neatly three, four times, before it straightens and glides down, hands out to catch a wall ledge like a bat before he executes a perfect back-flip onto a blue mat.

Oohs and ahhs erupt from members watching him, so he does a bow and flashes a smile. The smile that makes my throat catch and pulse race every time. For sure he knows I've arrived, but since he doesn't look right at me, I make myself busy changing my shoes.

"Encore, Sarfraz!" the instructor calls out as the preteen girls clap.

"Thanks, but I'm done for the day," Sarfraz replies, striding towards the rear door.

It's my signal, but I can't be too obvious, so I do a half-hearted warm-up followed by wall tic-tacs, then wait till the teacher is coaching some of the older teen boys before slipping out the same door.

Sarfraz lounges with back turned in the doorway of the Academy's storage shed, where we always meet. He's smoking a cigarette. Gross. I sneak up behind and circle my arms around his broad chest, totally unprepared for the elbow that whips back and connects with my stomach, throwing me to the ground.

"*Unnhhh.*" I look up at him, clutching my gut, lips trembling as pain bolts through me.

"Bronte!" he says in surprise, setting his cigarette down on the rusty chair beside us, his face red. "You shouldn't surprise me like that. Could have been a mugger." He leans down to help me up, though not as fast as I'd like.

"Sorry, Sarfraz," I manage to say with the little breath I have left. "I'd definitely think twice before mugging you." I force a little laugh, then brush myself off. Backing a few steps into the shadowy shed, I wait for the hug that will make up for the violence. Instead, he picks up his cigarette again and sucks on it for a while. It makes his kisses taste kind of bitter. But Arab boys don't take advice on such matters from girls, especially blond white girls they refuse to be seen with in public.

"Well?" he asks.

I take a deep breath. "We're leaving next week."

"So you said."

I try to hear sadness or regret in his flat tone but have to imagine it instead.

"It's for the best, Bronte. I'm leaving next week too."

"Leaving? Where?" Panic rises. This is where he's supposed to beg me to stay, or promise to call and write a lot. And why hasn't he told me before now that something or someone is messing with his world too?

"A training camp, sort of. My parkour skills have been noticed."

"That's great, Sarfraz," I say, perhaps too fast, too enthusiastically. "You've always been one of the best in the Academy. So this is with elite coaches and stuff? For how long?"

He tosses his cig to the ground, grinds it with the heel of his red trainer, and finally joins me inside the dark hut. He hesitates, then lifts a hand to push a lock of hair behind my ear.

"A head scarf would look good on you, Bronte. It would make you look more...modest."

Modest? I bite my tongue. We've had this discussion

before. I'm not Muslim. He knew that from the beginning. So why the eff would I wear a hijab? And why do this now, when we should be kissing goodbye?

I silently order his hand to remain touching my face. But it drops, and he looks to one side of me, all silent.

"Sarfraz?" My voice catches a little. *Stay strong, Bronte.* "We'll stay in touch, won't we?"

His eyes find their way back to me. "We're both on social media," he replies, shrugging. Then he turns towards the door and looks around, like he's afraid of being seen alone with me. Not like when we first met at the Academy, when he was so hot to offer me parkour tips, hear about my life in the United States, and sneak out here to touch my burning skin.

I grab his hands and pull him closer. "I'll miss you, Sarfraz. I... I..."

"You are a strong, resilient girl, and I am sure you will readjust fine. Shhh." He wraps his arms around me and finally puts his lips on mine, exploring my mouth with his tongue till I think I might dissolve. "It has been nice," he says, pulling away abruptly. "I'm going up to the roof."

Without waiting for an answer, he sprints out of the shed to the rear of the two-storey building next door to the Parkour Academy. There's no ladder, but traceurs (and traceuses, female traceurs) don't need ladders. He jumps up to grab a wall bracket, squeezes it with both hands, and uses it to lift his entire, gorgeously chiselled form with no effort, to a windowsill. Up he goes, his speed and grace putting Spider-Man to shame.

I'm the kind of girl who likes a challenge, and Sarfraz knows it. So soon I'm scrambling up to the roof after him. My breath is a little ragged as I near the cement rooftop, where he sits calm and cross-legged. His hand shoots out to help me with the last hoist. I ignore it and pull myself over the edge on my own, plop down beside him, then snuggle up close, but he doesn't lean in. Just points to a row of ships barely visible on the horizon.

"See those?"

"Yes," I say, realizing this is the last week I'll see the Abū Qīr Bay before returning to the USA.

"Part of the problem, not the solution." He speaks in English, something he's pretty proud of, though my Arabic is not too shabby.

"What do you mean?"

"Lots of them are smuggling ships. Anchored just past the line that means they are in international waters. Fishing boats that manage to dodge the Coast Guard shuttle people out there. People who think there's a better place to live than the Middle East."

I smart at the implication of the last sentence, and study the ships in the fading light. I've heard all about the smuggling operations. Who hasn't? So many tragedies: desperate people taking rickety, overcrowded vessels that sink and drown them all.

"And you're part of the solution?" I can't resist baiting him, though we never talk politics.

"I will be," he says, "after my camp."

I don't want to know what that means, so I reach for his hand, but it is busy lifting a pair of binoculars from a box sitting beside us up here on the roof.

"Yours?" I ask, surprised. "You come up here a lot?"

"Yes. I can spy on them, the groups of illegals that gather

along the beach near dark. You can see them now, sneaking down the alleyways from their crummy hotels and hideaway apartments. Look."

He hands the binoculars to me. I focus in as dusk descends. "I see a bunch of people headed to fishing boats waiting on the beach. But why are we talking about this?" I drop the binoculars, a little pissed off.

"It's like watching a sport, Bronte: The fastest get to the fishing boats first. The slowest get left behind on the beach. Not that any of that matters if the Coast Guard catches the skiffs before they reach international waters."

"What happens then?" I ask, thinking it's kind of creepy that he watches all this from up here.

"The smugglers throw them overboard to drown, so they can pretend to be fishermen and not get arrested or have their boats seized."

"That's warped. Please can we talk about something else, Sarfraz?"

"Oh, and some of the Coast Guard guys are double agents, as in they help so-called extremist recruiters find fighters from among the would-be escapees. No one is who they seem out there."

"Recruiters," I repeat with distaste.

He lowers the binoculars. "We've said goodbye, Bronte. There's nothing more to say. We're from two different worlds."

My body goes cold and slack. "That's—that's all?"

He stows the binoculars back in their box and lifts a hand to my shoulder—awkwardly, like we've only just met. "I've never known a girl who can do parkour like you. Goodbye, Bronte Miller."

A peck on the cheek, and then he rises and slides himself off the rooftop in one swift motion. Panicked, my heart breaking into a thousand pieces, I stand and run to the edge. Barely touching the ledges and sills on the way down, he descends two storeys, rolls, and runs into the gathering gloom.

CHAPTER THREE

"Hope your first day of school goes well," Mom says as she pulls the car up to Three Rivers High School.

Dad has been gone a few days, and Mom and I have called a ceasefire for the moment. Basically I'm too culture-shocked and jetlagged to function in fight mode, or any other mode. But I've vowed to make an effort today. To act normal, somehow. To convince myself I'm "home," though I feel as spinny as an astronaut crash-landing from space.

"I'm fine, Mom. Thanks for the ride." It's shameful that I talked her into a ride, really, when our house is within walking distance of school. The school, public library, and community centre all sit below twin bluffs that stand between us and the city's riverfront.

I open the car door and step out.

"Eeeek! It's Bronte!" a voice squeals.

I smile. Jazel Murphy, my best friend.

"Bronte! Bronte! Bronte!" other girls within hearing chant, jumping up and down and waving their arms.

Hey, they are the Three Rivers High School cheerleading squad, so how else would they greet their long-lost teammate? I rise from the car like the queen on a walkabout, wave to everyone, and then beeline to hug Jazel. Play your former self, I think. Maybe who you were will come back to you.

As Mom pulls away from the curb, they start in.

"How was Alexandria?"

"You look great!"

"Flashy top. Is that what they wear in Egypt?"

"Can't believe you're finally back!"

"At least you're not wearing a hijab or something."

"Oh my god, we were sooo worried about you over there!"

"Guess what? Cheerleading trials are next week and there's a party tonight at Natalie's—"

"Give the girl a break. She has barely landed!" Jazel says, running a black manicured fingernail through her long red hair, linking arms with me, and leading me towards the school.

More grateful than Jazel can imagine, I let her guide me into the building. It all feels so unreal, the half-familiar school corridors, lockers, and buzz in English. The girls in tight clothes, heads bare. The cloying smell of disinfectant and whiffs of perfume. I remind myself it took serious time to get used to my school in Alexandria a year ago. Was it really only one year ago?

You are a strong, resilient girl, and I'm sure you'll readjust fine. No! I mustn't think of Sarfraz, or I'll have some kind of meltdown right here in front of everyone.

"Bronte?" It's Jazel, staring at me with eyebrows slanting. "You okay? Looking a little spaced-out."

"I'm fine."

"I was saying we have first period together, computer science. The teacher's a new guy, Mr. Legendre, from France. Here's the cool thing, Bronte—he's *ooh-la-la* good-looking and into parkour. Even trained with Sébastien Foucan."

Foucan is a super-famous traceur originally from France and now big with Parkour UK.

"And—dah dah—" she makes sure she has my attention —"he now runs the parkour club in the community centre after school. Took it over this summer when Mr. Gleason moved away. Everyone is totally into him."

"Oh," I say, trying to take all that in. "Computer science. Not my best subject. Too bad he doesn't teach French." I'm good at languages. French, Arabic, English. I just need to not mix them all up today.

"Oh, and there are two new kids this year besides you."

"I'm not new," I say dryly.

"I know. So, some refugee guy from the Middle East— Pearl's cousin—and a total babe from Texas. Both are juniors like us."

"Hmm," I say, amused as ever by Jazel's enthusiasm, especially when it comes to the male of the species.

We enter a classroom, and I sink into a desk beside Jazel at the back. I try not to stare at Mr. Legend, or whatever his name is. He's a hot-looking black dude with a short beard and a smile that could land him in a toothpaste ad. Not to mention a body that could be, well, that of legendary parkour guru Foucan.

I start as the bell rings. We didn't have bells in my Alexandria high school.

"Good morning, class, and welcome to a new school year. I'm Julian Legendre, and this is computer science. Since I'm new to Three Rivers High School, I'll kick off by telling you three random things about myself, and then we're going to go around the room and each of you is going to do the same, so we get to know each other."

Groans, snickers. Does he think this is grade school? "Pretty touchy-feely for a computer class," I whisper to Jazel, but she's gazing starry-eyed at some tall, skinny guy with stringy black hair two rows across I've never seen before. And he's staring at *me*.

"So, I come from Paris, France," Legendre says. "My father was a computer science professor when computers were the size of rooms." A few laughs. "And my interests outside of computer science are philosophy, religion, and—"

"—parkour!" Jazel shouts out.

He smiles big, and I see why my friend and fellow traceuse tagged him *ooh-la-la*, though he's too old and not my type.

"Confirmed by one of my parkour students, yes," Mr. Legendre says. "Okay, let's go down the rows. Tell us three things about yourself you'd like to share, though we won't make you if you don't want to participate."

"Hi. I'm Tommy Fox, or Foxy Tom, if you prefer," says a classmate I've known forever, a short guy with a peach-fuzz moustache sitting at the front of the room. "My favourite things in life are baseball, pizza, bowling, and watching thrillers. Oh, and last year I started parkour, the only French thing I'm into besides French fries."

Ha Ha. Can't get more all-American than Tommy Fox. And it's good he's trying out parkour.

I yawn as the contributions continue, tedious voices stating things I already know, because most of us have known each other since preschool.

Still, when the new, tall, black-haired thin guy speaks, I sit up almost as straight as Jazel. "Hi, I'm Dan Lyon, and my family just moved here from Lubbock, Texas. I like blondes and fast cars. I'm looking forward to getting to know y'all." It's a southern drawl quickly mimicked in whispers. I frown as he turns to look directly at me, and shrug when Jazz gives me a puzzled look, like, "Do you know him or something?"

Hmm, we need to change his tastes from blondes to redheads.

The rounds continue—using up clock time, I remind myself. Only six hours to go till school's out, and I can crawl back into bed. Jetlag sucks.

"I'm Karam Saif," comes a soft voice with an Arabic accent.

I swing around, not having noticed the other new boy till now.

"I've just moved here from Yemen and am living with my cousin, Pearl."

Yemen, seriously?

"Where's Yemen?" Dan asks bluntly. "In Africa?"

Texan Fast-Cars Boy isn't going to pull As in Geography, I decide.

"It's on the Arabian Peninsula across a strait from Africa," Karam replies patiently.

He's olive-skinned, kind of handsome, and very fit-looking. Though, nowhere near as hot as Sarfraz. From the set of his face and shoulders, I sense a sadness and wonder what his story is, given Yemen's horrifying state at the moment. Perhaps his whole family just arrived as refugees and is crowded in with Pearl's?

"Arab, huh? Does that make you a Muslim?" Dan asks in

a snarky voice, sitting tall like he's convinced he's impressing people.

I cringe. There's an awkward silence for a second. Karam looks a little unsure how to respond, and Mr. Legendre moves towards Dan, opening his mouth to speak, but it's Pearl who replies first.

"Yes, we're Muslim."

Though I've gone to school with Pearl since second grade —that's when she and her family first came here from Yemen —I hardly know the girl at all. Let's just say she's the shyest student at Three Rivers. As far as I know, neither she nor her family mix with anyone outside the tiny Muslim community here. She doesn't do extracurricular school stuff, for sure— I've never even seen her attend a school concert or game.

I remember feeling sorry for her three years ago, when she started wearing a hijab. She got a lot of flak from our less-than-enlightened student body. And I kind of respected her for handling the stupid questions and bullying in her own quiet but assertive way.

"Do you wear that in the shower?"

"No, we remove them when we enter our house."

"Like, your brothers and uncles can see your hair then?"

"If I had brothers or uncles, yes, because they'd be family."

"Why do you dress like that when you're in the US now?"

"For the same reason you wear that cross around your neck and don't go to school in a bikini: modesty and respect for our faith."

"Oh" is how those conversations usually end.

All I really know about Pearl is that she's wicked smart. I've also heard she's a respected teen leader at her mosque.

"Bronte?" Jazel is elbowing me like she has caught me in a trance again. "Your turn."

"Oh. I'm Bronte Miller. I was born and raised here. I like languages, and I'm useless at computer science." That prompts a few giggles. "When I graduate, I want to run a parkour gym for kids."

"Right on!" says Dan, but it's Karam's face I notice turn and study mine. His head tips slightly to one side like he's puzzled. I know there are parkour clubs all over the Middle East, but I'm guessing that Yemen, being more conservative than many countries there, doesn't have females who do parkour.

"That's it for introductions," Mr. Legendre says. He launches into a lecture about the influence of the internet on society, then says, "Now we're going to break into six-person groups and prepare presentations for next class on how the internet has affected life, both positively and negatively."

Before Jazel and I can nab four other cheerleader types to form our own little pack, Mr. Legendre is pointing fingers and dictating who's going to work with whom. I sigh as I find myself in a circle with Jazel, Texas Dan, Karam, Pearl, and Tommy.

"Hey, Dan and Karam. Welcome to Three Rivers High," Tommy kicks off, high-fiving them.

"Thanks, buddy," Dan says to Tommy, our would-be Welcome Wagon guy. Tommy's hard not to like. He's always upbeat and good to people.

"Thank you," Karam echoes, smiling wide.

"I'll start," Dan announces. "I say the internet makes it way easier for terrorists to operate in our country." He locks eyes on Karam and Pearl.

"It also makes it easier for intelligence agencies to track down terrorists," Karam says evenly.

I find it interesting that Karam is fluent in English. Must come from a rich family that put him in an international school in Yemen, where classes would be in English.

"Good for downloading movies," Tommy speaks up.

"It helps people connect up socially," Jazel says, throwing eyelash-batting side glances at Dan.

"It's useful for research so that people operate on facts and not assumptions," Pearl contributes.

"It has great YouTube clips on cheerleading moves," I weigh in, winking at Jazel.

"Cheerleading moves? That's what you use the internet for?" Karam asks, one eyebrow raised.

"And why wouldn't I, being a cheerleader?" I snap. It's not like I'm going to tell him I watch news clips about Yemen obsessively, hoping to glimpse my father in order to combat my nightmares of him getting injured or killed. I hardly sleep at all the nights I don't see him.

"What else do you use the internet for?" Dan asks me in an overly interested tone, leaning my way.

"Cookie recipes, hip-hop music, porn, and bubble-bath product reviews," I lie, now that I'm on a roll.

Pearl and Jazel are trying not to laugh. Dan is studying me for clues on how to react.

Stupid, shallow blonde, Karam mutters in Arabic.

Gullible, arrogant newcomer, I toss back in Arabic. *Chill, or you're not going to make friends around here.*

As his mouth drops open, Pearl whirls around. "You learned Arabic in Egypt?" They are some of the only words she has ever spoken to me.

Her cousin's face has gone eggplant-purple, and he's looking out the window like he's about to leap out.

"Yes," I reply. "And from my dad before we left."

"But you said you grew up here," says Dan.

"I also said I like languages. Now, are we going to do this class assignment or not? Pearl, why don't you take notes...?"

CHAPTER FOUR

"Hey, everyone, it's the seldom-seen Bronte come to run with us!"

Jazel's teasing is deserved, of course. I've missed a couple of parkour sessions, even some school classes lately, just because of lack of energy. It couldn't be jetlag anymore. It's exhaustion. I shake uncontrollably every evening when the news comes on. Mom doesn't join me. And then, instead of sleeping at night, I lie in bed, my face weakly lit by my laptop, searching for anything about Yemen I can find. I picture Dad being where a bomb created a house-sized crater next to a hospital, or him interviewing civilians while masked terrorists sneak up behind him.

Plus, every morning, I spend half an hour tapping out messages to Sarfraz, then waste half the day looking for the replies that never come. Worse, I trudge home from school each afternoon with shoulders tensed for fights with Mom. It's like we're locked in a Cold War of our own. Neighbours several doors down have probably heard all our shouting matches. I'm so tired and bent out of shape that I shocked all my cheerleader friends by dropping out of cheerleading yesterday. But I'd never quit parkour.

"Come to run with you? You mean run you into the ground," I retort, forcing a grin. "Am I the last one here?"

"You are. We held off just for you," Mr. Legendre says. "Okay with doing the western butte up to the top for the river view, then back down here again?"

"Times two," I declare, looking around and counting a dozen students doing warm-up stretches. Five from the cheerleading squad, including Jazel, Natalie Llanos, and me. Tommy, Karam the Yemini boy, the new Texan pain-in-the-butt Dan, Vansh, Ryker, and a few others who offer no threat to my taking the lead. Er, my former self taking the lead. For sure I've been losing my fitness edge, but intend to sweat off my drowsiness today, run it into the ground.

"Hey, Bronte," Dan greets me. "Just so you know, I've never done parkour before, but it sounds like the parkour club is the thing to join in this town. Anyway, I figured I'd come along today."

"Whatever," I say neutrally.

"Bronte!" Vansh and Ryker greet me together.

Vansh is someone I admire, because he's constantly pushing the envelope with parkour moves. Ryker, on the other hand, is a cocky, long-haired boy I avoid because of his reputation for B&Es and other activities that make the police suspicious of our entire club.

"Hey, guys. Good to be back," I say.

"Heard from your Egyptian hottie?" Jazel asks, striding along beside me, red hair flying in the breeze, as the group starts moving.

"Shhh," I snap, wondering if I should have told her anything at all. "No. Nothing. But he's at a parkour camp, so maybe they're not allowed internet access." I'm not really so out of it that I believe it's a traceur camp. I'm all too aware what kind of training camp Sarfraz might have gotten himself into. But what's the point of worrying, if he won't even answer my messages?

"Hmm, I say move on. He's not worth it," my friend advises. "Lots of BAE's this side of the world. But"—she drops her voice to a conspiratorial whisper—"hands off Dan. He's all mine."

You're welcome to him, I'm tempted to say, but instead I just mumble, "Go for it, Jazz." Then an unwelcome thought enters my mind: Has Jazel changed over the past year, or have I? She doesn't seem like best-friend-material so much as before.

Natalie catches up, her dark curly hair tucked into a pink baseball cap. "How's your dad?" she asks in her high, breathless voice.

I pick up the pace to put our threesome's conversation beyond the hearing range of Legendre, whose long, lithe legs are keeping him too close behind us.

"He doesn't get regular access to internet or phone," I report, "but he lets us know he's alive now and again, and I've seen some of his reports on TV."

"Exciting job," Natalie says, since she's too polite to say *freakin' dangerous job*. "So, I got the details on this Karam guy," she continues proudly, keeping up with my killer pace all too easily.

"Okay, spill," I say, curious but glancing back to make sure no one else is within hearing.

"Family all drowned trying to get out of Africa."

"Middle East, if you mean Yemen," I correct her, my chest constricting out of sympathy for him, or maybe from trying to outpace my fellow cheerleaders.

"Whatever. That's soooo sad. And he seems kind of shy. Won't even look at me when I try to talk with him."

"That's 'cause you wear such skanky outfits," I tease Natalie. "He probably finds what you wear indecent. Anyway, it's tradition and a form of politeness in conservative Muslim communities for men to not look directly at women."

"Ha! Like you and this Egyptian parkour star I've been hearing about?" she tosses back.

I give Jazel the evil eye.

"Hey, no secrets on the squad," Jazz counters, but I can see a flash of guilt on her face. So much for trusting her with confidential information.

"Ready to pick it up?" Legendre's deep voice is right behind us.

I grit my teeth, fearing he heard most of our conversation. No secrets on the squad, as if. More like no secrets at Three Rivers High.

"Hang back a minute," I whisper to Jazz and Natalie, pretending it's about letting Legendre and the guys get ahead and out of earshot, when really it might be about my lagging lung power.

"So this Karam guy," Natalie is saying. "He must be pretty religious, 'cause that over-the-top Muslim girl, Pearl—"

"Pearl's okay," I defend her. "Why is she over the top? Just 'cause she prays five times a day, at specific times, which is what all Muslims are supposed to do?" Truth is, I never really bothered the past year to learn much about Muslims. That's about all I know. But even having lived there just a year, I'm feeling like a fish out of water here now.

"Yeah, and gets special permission to leave the classroom to do it, and gets a special room for it," Natalie protests in her whiny voice. "Anyway, she's like sooo proud of this new cousin. She hardly says a word, ever, but now she's telling everyone that Karam the Superhero is going to be holding a public information session on Islam soon, with special permission of the Ee-mom."

"Imam," I correct her. "That's what they call their religious leaders. Same as a priest, minister, or rabbi. So? It might be interesting."

"Why, you going to convert to get your boyfriend back?" she hurls at me. "And what are you, Richland's new expert on all things Muslim?"

"Of course not!" I stop and stare at her, floored by the challenging tone. That's a warning, I tell myself. No more revealing anything I know about the stupid Middle East.

"Time out, Bronte and Nat," says Jazz, moving closer to Natalie and giving me a weird look.

"Girls, girls, this is a training run, not a coffee break," says Legendre, who somehow has managed to drop back to our sphere without my noticing. "Put the energy in your lungs into moving, not talking, *mes filles*" [my girls].

"I second that," I say, and power up with every cell in my body. Run, run away from my narrow-minded friends, away from memories of Sarfraz, away from worries about Dad, away from Legendre's snoopy ears. Push, push past easy, past hard, past howling pain. Show them what you can still do.

How's my American star? Come to wow us with one of

your high-velocity workouts? I cover my ears to drown out my Egyptian parkour instructor's voice, and try to block the memory of Sarfraz's last kiss. I gun it up the hill, passing a surprised Tommy and Karam—chatting away like they've totally bonded, which is nice—then Dan, who tries to up his pace to chat with me. Sweat streams off me as I pour on enough to leave him in my dust.

My calves are cramping, my lungs are killing me, and my hamstrings are locked up like paralyzed pistons. Still, the memories of Sarfraz, and Dad and Mom's fights in Egypt, torture my brain. Plus, I'm feeling uncomfortably hot. Like, seriously overheated. In need of a fire hose before I spontaneously combust. My ankles threatening to buckle, I stagger to the top of the butte, slump onto the bench there, and pause, gasping.

I'm facing north, drinking in the view of the meandering river and our puny but panoramic city. To my right is a forty-foot vertical drop-off into a narrow ravine from which a lone, determined red maple tree rises to about nine feet across from me. Six feet beyond its denuded upper trunk lies the eastern butte. People in our city like to joke that the eastern and western buttes are twins separated at birth by the deep gully that runs north to the river.

This is where we generally turn around and head back down the way we came. But feeling like an overheated engine, sweat streaming down my forehead, I look towards the wide river at the northern foot of this huge hump of dry dirt. Yes! Water. The river's cold this time of year, but that's what I need.

With no particular plan, I sprint down the far slope of the butte, through suburban neighbourhoods and across a busy road to river's edge, where I stagger onto a half-rotted pier and plunge in. The beautiful, shocking water cools my bod and flash-freezes my brain, temporarily deleting the memories and fears. I dive deep—deep enough to escape the world—

And then like a torpedo, Sarfraz shoots in beside me. One of his strong arms hooks loosely around my neck, pulling me gently but firmly to the surface. Strangely accepting his presence, I relax against his abs, and as we surface, allow him to tow me towards shore. I nestle my head against his, breathe in his scent, feel the sparks we always generate. They're there in force.

"Bronte!" Jazel is screaming, leaping about hysterically on the end of the warped pier. "Bronte, are you okay?"

I twist around and see not Sarfraz but Karam, his elbow around my neck.

"I've got you, Jaleela," he's saying, wild-eyed like he's half out of his mind.

I punch him hard, panicked. "What are you doing? Get your hands off me! Who the hell's Jaleela, anyway?"

Silence for a second. Then, "my younger sister," he mumbles.

His sister who drowned with the rest of his family trying to escape from Yemen? I bite my tongue.

As our toes touch the muddy bottom, he pulls away, the shock on his face probably mirroring my own. Then he loses the scary crazed look, and glances around like he has just returned to the real world and realizes what he has done.

"Bronte!" Mr. Legendre shouts, peeling off his track jacket to wrap me in. "What were you thinking?"

"I w-wanted a cool-down," I stutter, looking at a circle of faces studying mine.

Tommy removes the sweatshirt tied around his waist and

offers it to soaking-wet Karam, who is totally failing to hide his shivering.

"You're one crazy chick," Dan declares, shaking his head at me.

"I needed a polar-bear swim," I say, standing tall. "I didn't need a wannabe hero rescuing me. You scared me half to death, Karam. Lucky you didn't drown us both."

"Sorry, sorry," he mutters. "I shouldn't have—"

"Okay, kids, huddle in the picnic shelter over here," Legendre is saying, "and the rest of you keep these two wet maniacs warm, while I bring my van around. I would say it has been a good run, but it certainly had a curious ending." He looks at me like he's worried about my mental state.

I could tell him that I'm perfectly fine, and nothing is wrong with cooling off after a hard run, even in October. Instead I shrug and say, "I think I won, hey? Fastest of the fast? Thanks for the coat, Mr. L. Very gentlemanly of you."

Whoa, pretty snark even for me, but offence is the best defence, right? As for Karam, I give him a withering look that tells him he'd better stay clear. I'm burning with embarrassment about the Sarfraz vision, and even more—like, way more—about something else: the sparks. Sparks I felt for a moment even after I knew it was Karam, not Sarfraz. Sparks I've denied feeling when around the new kid before.

Mom stands with eyes blazing and arms folded on our front steps. She shoves a towel at me as I step inside, Mr. Legendre having called before driving me home.

"You actually jumped into a freezing-cold river after a long run, when you knew you had no spare clothes or towel? And someone had to dive in to rescue you? I swear you're not right in the head since we got back from Egypt. I've got a bath running."

"I swear you weren't right in the head in Alexandria," I retort, "abandoning Dad."

"You watch how you talk to me, young lady," Mom says, hands on her hips. "I know you're angry, but your father and I are working things out, and that's all that matters."

"Working things out? What, by email to Yemen?"

"Drop it," Mom warns. "I don't want to fight, Bronte. I do want to know why you jumped into the river, especially given all the sick days you've been taking lately."

"It's called a cold-water cure, Mom. I'll be right as rain tomorrow." I mimic her favourite old-fashioned phrase in a mocking tone.

"Bronte, seriously, you're not yourself lately. This erratic behaviour worries me. I can't believe you've dropped cheer-leading, too."

"I'd be myself if Dad came home. As in, if you hadn't driven him away." And if Sarfraz contacted me.

She looks like she's going to snap at me, but purses her lips and straightens her back. "Have you considered talking to a counsellor, Bronte? You seem to have anger issues, and you're sad and tired a lot. I don't know why you even went for a run."

"To get away from the person who wrecked our family."

That does it. Mom's face kind of crumples, and she turns on her heel and heads for her bedroom. She closes rather than slams the door. Two points for that. Fine. Guess it's bath time. I undress in the bathroom and slide into the filled tub, tears running down my cheeks.

I'm a rotten, rude person. I'm not supposed to hate my mother or treat her like that. When did I become such a monster? Why is my life falling apart? And what am I supposed to do about it?

A flashback of Karam diving in and hauling me to shore forces itself on me. Gentle, shy, kind Karam. Handsome as hell, if I had to admit it. And I treated him like absolute shit. Time for some major changes in my life.

CHAPTER FIVE

"So Karam," says Tommy, "this is your official initiation to Richland."

Tommy, Karam, Ryker, Jazel, and I are squeezed into a pink vinyl booth with a Formica table in an over-bright place called Bubba's Burgers, which smells of grease and potatoes. I'm determined to keep my mouth shut and sit a good distance away from Karam, but maybe also find a chance to apologize to him about the river thing.

"Initiation," Karam echoes, smiling shyly like he's delighted that half the parkour team is going to show him around town this afternoon.

"First, we're in this fine fast-food joint to ingest French fries, a hamburger, and some sickly sweet drink," Tommy continues as Jazel and Ryker grin and I roll my eyes. "Then we're going to a bowling alley, and you're going to learn how to knock pins down, and then we're attending a slasher movie. Got it?"

"And I'm not supposed to ask what a slasher movie is?"

"Exactly."

"Couldn't translate that if I wanted to," I mumble without looking at him.

Tommy punches Karam in the arm, so Karam grins and punches him back, a little awkwardly. As the server delivers our orders, I lift my bun and study the pickle and double layer of meat. What would Karam's aunt and uncle say if they knew Tommy had just ordered Karam

a meal involving animals killed without the blessing of Allah or in a way that they suffer minimal pain, the way Islam specifies? But no way I'm saying anything. Karam lifts his burger to his mouth and bites into it hungrily. One side glance at him and I sense that above all, he's determined to fit in, blend in, make friends. To be a real American, whatever he thinks that is.

"Tell me how you got into parkour," Tommy says, pausing in the midst of wolfing down his own burger.

"YouTube," Karam replies. "Some friends and I started copying the motions, and then we formed a group and got good at it. We practised constantly, made up our own moves, and got strong and fluid. It kept us sane during the—well, Yemen has a civil war going on. So just getting outside for exercise can be a challenge there. During ceasefires, my friends and I would go out—"

"Out onto the streets in the middle of a war zone?" I speak up, horrified from having seen clips of my Dad there surrounded by abandoned tanks and collapsed buildings. "How bad was it?" Oops, I was going to keep quiet.

He studies the table for a minute, then seems to gather up his words and courage.

"One day, during a ceasefire, I crawled out of the basement of our apartment building, where we'd been hiding with lots of other families for days. I went to check on our top-floor apartment from the curb outside. The left half of it was lopped off and lying in rubble on the street, as if a giant machete had sliced it in two. All the windowpanes were shattered, with bits of orange satin curtains poking out of them. The exterior walls that still existed were pockmarked by bullet holes. The living room was totally exposed, our blue velvet sofa with one leg thrust into mid-air, as if it wanted to do a daring high-dive."

"Seriously?" Ryker asks, burger halfway to his mouth.

"Yes. I sprang up the inside stairs three at a time, fingers tracing a line in the dust along the brass spiral railing. The crystal chandelier over the lobby lay smashed on the marble floor. Glass nuggets shone like diamonds on the tiles, too pretty to be swept up.

"When I reached our apartment, I knew we were lucky. The rear bedrooms were still okay, as if Allah had chosen that we sleep comfortably that night. It required only a few tarps."

Everyone in the Bubba's booth has gone very quiet.

"And your parents were okay with your doing parkour in the middle of all that?" I ask.

He nods like it's a reasonable question.

"After my buddies and I spent eight hours moving debris and freeing trapped families around our neighbourhood, Dad said go ahead and take a break."

Jazel lowers her burger to her plate. Everyone's eyes are fixed on Karam.

"First, it was a warm-up run through the park, dodging lifted slabs of concrete. Then we reached an open plaza, and it was time for some show-off aerial stunts, done from a running position. I tested out my tumbling by cartwheeling into a high-dive roll, and warmed up with a few butterfly kicks before throwing a butterfly twist. It was like high-fiving the fresh air of our tarnished but still beautiful city."

Still beautiful city. I've seen pictures of Aden, and it is. Or was. I clench my teeth as I contemplate Dad there, moving through the torn-up streets, interviewing glassy-eyed victims of violence.

Meanwhile, Karam's face has gone dreamy, like he has left us and returned to his friends.

"Then we were moving as fast as the sea breeze, smooth and focused, every would-be obstacle beckoning like a prop eager to help us spin, jump, and fly.

"We found some blackened tanks and vaulted up and over, one after another of us. We were like hyped-up ballet dancers in T-shirts and sweats, dropping off the gun points onto the ground, rolling neatly to absorb the impact, springing up and proceeding to a brick building with blown-out arched windows. After waving to a soldier, we flew like ninjas through the window holes, tackling every one, like a woven chain of bodies darting in and out."

"W-what did the soldier do?" Tommy asks.

"He lowered his gun and stared at us because he was probably jealous, and then we just carried on."

I can't help smiling at the picture he's painting.

"Were there people around? Were they like staring at you?" Ryker wants to know.

"Yes, pedestrians would slow and watch, some open-mouthed, some smiling just a little. They'd shake their heads, wondering why a stream of grinning boys was hell-bent on vaulting over every crumbling wall in sight, and leaping with outstretched arms over trash-filled ditches. Why would we veer deliberately towards fields of rubbish, scorched cars, and twisted railings?"

"Yeah, why?" Tommy echoed.

"You know what we were really doing," Karam says in a triumphant voice, returning to the present and looking at each of us in turn. "We were absorbing the aftermath of the fight, neutralizing the ugly remnants, demonstrating that we could rise above and flow past anything."

"Huh?" mumbles Ryker.

"In the 1960s, peace-and-love American hippies stuck flowers into the gun barrels of riot police, right?"

"Um, yes," I say.

"We have the same power. I believe parkour teaches us to incorporate unexpected obstacles without losing stride. It teaches flexibility and resilience and acceptance," Karam says quietly.

"I get it," Tommy says. "The metaphysical side of parkour."

Tommy knows the word metaphysical? Who'd've thought?

"So," Tommy continues, "you're into the martial arts, quasi-meditation thing. Legendre talks about that a lot. He's kind of a philosophical dude."

"Where is Yemen, anyway?" Jazel asks, half apologetically.

"It's the southernmost tip of the Arabian Peninsula," Karam says. "Saudi Arabia lies on our north border. To our south is 150 miles of water stretching to the horn of Africa. I lived in Aden, right on the sparkling ocean. It's a busy seaport in an extinct volcanic crater. My father used to call the crater 'a dimple like Jaleela's.' She was one of my sisters. Unfortunately, Yemen doesn't have much oil like our neighbours. So for the moment, we're the poorest, most screwed-up country in the Arabian Peninsula, worse than Syria."

"What a drag," says Ryker. "Lucky you had relatives here to help you get out. So, it's like two sides fighting to run the country?"

"Worse. It's two sides plus a couple of terrorist groups all fighting each other. Very complicated." He hesitates, as if wondering if he has said too much.

It's not easy explaining the Middle East and its troubles, and I'm sure not going to butt in, or Jazel will start in about my dad.

"So, like, Muslim terrorists are a threat to Muslims?" That's Ryker again.

I manage not to sigh or shake my head over his naïve understatement. Good luck with that one, Karam. The rest of us busy ourselves with our soft drinks.

"The vast majority of Muslims are not extremists," he says patiently. "The extremists target those of us who are 'normal' Muslims way more than they do non-Muslim people. So I've never understood why Westerners think that those of us running away from them are extremists ourselves."

"Hmm, got a point there," Tommy says. "Anyway, sucks your country's at war. And I heard you lost your family on the way over. I'm really sorry for you, man. That info is all around the school now, you know, which maybe is better, because it means no one will ask you awkward questions. Hopefully it'll even make people friendlier. Ignore our guy Dan, by the way. Every community has its token headass."

Karam nods as if vaguely comforted. "And you, Tommy? When did you start doing parkour?"

"Just last year. I kind of suck at it. But like Dan said the other day, it's the club to join around here. I like the people in it. I'm not like Vansh, who's as pliable as Play-Doh and fast as a cheetah. He wants to be a stuntman."

"What's Play-Doh?"

I attempt to translate but end up giggling behind my hand.

"Never mind. Anyway, everyone in the club is here for a different reason, far as I can tell. Mr. Legendre was in the army—some say Secret Service in Afghanistan. You probably already know that's how parkour started, as military training."

"Yes, in France."

"Then there's Jazel, who's kind of a fitness freak."

"As if!" Jazel protests with a laugh.

"And Natalie, who's into photography and always posting clips of our group online. Ryker here likes to keep fit enough to outrun police."

"Hey don't tell him all our secrets," Ryker retorts, laughing, before vacuuming up his ketchup-soaked onion rings.

"What's your angle, Karam?" Ryker asks. "You're pretty hot shit from what I've seen."

"Thanks. I like the flow, the challenge of keeping it smooth. I find it so absorbing that I forget about—"

"—about the crappy stuff in your life," I speak up before turning seriously red.

"And you, Bronte?" Karam asks softly, chestnut eyes turning to me.

When I hesitate, Tommy steps in for me. "Bronte's like a super-amazing traceuse. Way better than any of us. She could really go somewhere with parkour."

"I just like it," I say lamely. "It's something I have to do." And it really does help me forget the crappy side of my life for awhile.

A phone buzz has us all checking our pockets.

"Sorry," Karam says, lifting his.

"No worries. Take it," Tommy says, leaning back and cupping his hands behind his messy brown hair. We fumble for cash to pay our bills.

Karam's face whitens as he stares at the text—unless I'm imagining that.

"Who is RL?" he mumbles.

"RL stands for Richland," I inform him. "Our city. Are you okay?"

"No caller ID, and it won't let me reply," Karam says, working his thumbs.

"Spam. Ignore it," Tommy says. "Now, about the bowling alley."

"I'm ready," Karam says overloud, pocketing his phone like it's infected, which is definitely kind of strange.

CHAPTER SIX

"HA! YOU KIDS ALL BUT SLEPT THROUGH CLASS TODAY," Legendre teases us on Monday afternoon at the community centre. He's wearing his usual spotless navy-blue track suit. "I suspect you were out carousing last night. But you're good for parkour?"

"We were busy Americanizing Karam," Tommy informs our teacher, slapping Karam on the back.

"I always have enough energy for parkour," I say, though it's true I'm done-in this afternoon. All that time with the group last night, and I never did remember to apologize to Karam, damn it.

"Well, come join us on the floor. We're teaching Dan some basics, Vansh is trying to kill himself with some new moves I haven't approved, and the girls are doing their own thing in the far corner."

I look over and see Vansh on top of a narrow ledge, stretching and eyeing a pole ten feet across the room and posing like he's about to do a cat leap. No way. Can't make that, Vansh. Going to hurt yourself.

Farther over, Jazel is doing a running jump. She arcs through the air, clearing two vault boxes, then softly sticks a landing on a narrow railing. Nice one, girl. Natalie's warming up beside Jazel.

"Karam," Mr. Legendre calls out. "Could you spot for Dan a minute? He's trying to do a backflip."

"Of course," Karam says, moving that way.

"I said I could do it myself," Dan says with a flash of irritation.

Oh, get over yourself, Dan, I want to say.

He whips his head back and does a sloppy back-tuck as he takes off from a ledge, then under-rotates and lands on all fours, nearly hitting his face against the dense foam floor.

Stubborn smartass.

"Try focusing on something straight in front of you. It'll help keep you more upright as you take off," Karam suggests.

"Hey, Bronte," Dan calls out louder. "Mr. Legendre thinks I need a hand. Come give me a lift?"

"We're busy," Natalie shouts, putting a restraining hand on Jazel, who seems about to bounce over. "Later?"

"Just listen to Karam," I say, lifting a foot to a bar to stretch my calf muscles.

"Karam's right," says Tommy, stepping forward to place his hand on Dan's lower back. "Just lean back a touch, look straight ahead, and keep your chin tucked. I'll spot for you."

Dan shrugs, lets Tommy move into place, and once again whips his head back and does an awkward, low back-tuck. Thanks to Tommy's spotting, the Texan novice manages to land feet first for a minute before needing to put his hands out to catch himself.

"You'll get it. Just keep trying," Karam says.

"Nah, done for the day," Dan declares, and he stalks past his helpers to the men's shower room. Totally snubbing them.

"Okay, Karam, show me how to do an Arabian," Tommy requests with a teasing grin, to break the tension.

Karam chuckles and shows him how the set—the takeoff —for an Arabian begins like that for a backflip, except both hands start at one hip and cross the body upwards, twisting the body ninety degrees before it's time to initiate the front tuck that finishes the move.

Legendre's eyebrows shoot up, and he breaks into an appreciative smile as Tommy starts practising the set, and dive-rolling out of it.

"Like, wow," Natalie mumbles, almost reluctantly. "He's amazing."

Amazing? More like genius, I think. Move over, Foucan.

Tommy does a few more practice sets, then warms up his standing fronts. Both look solid.

"Okay," Karam encourages him, "try a full move."

"Yeah, Tommy, go for it!" I encourage them, not about to steal any fire by performing it myself yet.

Legendre nods his approval.

Tommy manages to land his off a low vault box onto a shallow mat, while Jazz and Natalie start practising their Arabians at ground level. For the next fifteen minutes, we all give the session our full energy.

"Hey Karam," Natalie eventually calls out, "want to do some synchronized tumbling?"

"Sure," he tosses back easily.

Now it's Tommy, us cheerleaders, and Karam chasing around the gym like there's a pack of wolves after us. We jump, flip, laugh, and roll. Legendre puts on some music, and we make like a high-speed dance troupe. Finally we collapse into a sweaty pile on a blue mat in the middle of the gym.

"Wow, that was fun," Natalie declares, sweaty curls framing her smiling face. "Hey, Karam and Tommy, I'm having a party Saturday night at my house. Parents are outta town. Wanna come?"

"Always good for a Natalie party," Tommy declares, "and Karam here needs to experience one to qualify as a real Three Rivers High School guy."

"Yes!" Jazel and Natalie exclaim together, beaming.

Karam hesitates and glances at me, prompting my lungs to miss a breath. I realize he's waiting for something, so I look at him and smile. "Be brave. Say yes," I instruct him in Arabic. The language bond is definitely something we both feel. Besides, his being Arab has upped my interest in learning more about Middle East culture. Truth is, I'm kind of ashamed I never paid much attention over there.

"I accept," Karam says. "By the way, Saturday morning my cousin Pearl and I are doing a seminar on Islam here at the community centre. We would love you all to come."

Perfect, I think. I'd be into that. Might make up for a growing feeling that I don't fit into my former scene here anymore.

"Interesting," Jazel says too brightly. "Well, I'll think about it."

Natalie's smile fades, and she bounces up and pulls off her wrist bands. "Have other plans, but Tommy knows my address, so see you Saturday night. It's BYOB."

"What's BYOB?" Karam whispers to Tommy.

Tommy laughs. "Bring your own booze. Do Muslims drink alcohol?"

"No," Karam says uneasily.

"Well, the party could change that," Tommy teases. "Or you could just bring something non-alcoholic."

"Lots of people do that," I reassure him.

"Nice of them to ask us," Karam says, eyes on his feet. "I've never been to a mixed party before."

"Whoa, way past time to check off that box, Kazam."

"Who?"

"Kazam. My new nickname for you. 'Cause when it comes to parkour, you move as fast as a 'pow! wham! kazam!' cartoon character. But trust me," Tommy says as he slings a long arm across Karam's sweaty shoulders, "you need a chaperone when it comes to Natalie's parties and other dangers of the Wild West." He whacks our club mate on the back. "Okay, time to head to Freezy Treats after we hit the showers."

Oops, Bronte you idiot, I realize. You still didn't manage an apology.

CHAPTER SEVEN

It's a cold and rainy Saturday morning. The community centre doors have just opened, and I'm waiting on the pavement outside, half hiding under my umbrella in the downpour. I'm excited to learn whatever the seminar might offer, but also hoping I won't get a hard time about it from school mates.

No one is going in or coming out yet, but there are a handful of protesters on the wet pavement waving signs.

One is tall and wearing a baseball cap over stringy black hair. No way. Dan? He's carrying a sign that says "Islam is evil!"

I shake my head and sigh.

"Bronte!" I hear Pearl's surprised, pleased voice. "I'm so glad you came," she says, linking her arm in mine and drawing me towards the doors.

I stare at her arm, shocked she'd do that. She's always so shy at school, such a total loner. And yet, she has always carried herself with a certain confidence, I have to admit, something I'm not feeling so much of these days.

"Karam is setting up inside. He's way nervous," she confides with a smile. "This was all his idea, you know. But of course the imam approved it."

"Oh," I say, wishing I'd worn more deodorant. My sweat glands are on overdrive.

"Bronte!" I hear Dan call out. "Come join our protest! Don't go through those doors with that Muslim girl! Don't listen to their lies!"

I lift my umbrella and glare at Dan but lack the energy to reply.

"Who do you think will come?" I ask Pearl, as we slip through the doors past the shouts and raised fists. Hopefully, no one else I know.

"No idea. It's in Room 8," she says, after we've shaken out our umbrellas.

We walk down the quiet corridor to the room, and I breathe easier once I step inside. It's empty. She lowers a backpack she's wearing and unzips it to reveal a bunch of brochures and a package of cookies. I help her set them up on a back table, wondering where Karam is and how he'll react to my being here. And whether anyone will show up.

"The pamphlets are in English. Though I'd love to help you practise your Arabic sometime if you're open to that."

"Um, thanks. Is your imam coming?" I ask as a bulky Middle-Eastern-looking man with an ugly face-scar walks in and slumps into a chair at the very back.

"Yes, but that's not the imam. It's the masjid's caretaker," she whispers. "He's also the youth leader, but I find him not very friendly. The imam plans to slip in at the last second and sit quietly at the back, so he doesn't make Karam nervous. He wants it to be about young people."

I agree with her that the caretaker is kind of intimidating, and take a back seat as far away from the guy as I can. I watch three, four, six people wander in, and then Karam appears from a side door, walking slowly and studying some notes. Pearl approaches him, leans in, and says something. Karam looks directly over at me. I stiffen but give him an encouraging smile. My blood's pumping like I'm doing a workout. To my relief, he smiles back. God, he's good-looking when he smiles. Note to self: Make the guy smile more often.

In fact, he's drop-dead gorgeous in dress trousers, white shirt, and tie. But these are not thoughts I'm supposed to be having. Nor am I supposed to be feeling a buzz just from being in the same room as him. At least he's not upset that I showed up. I came to finally apologize about the way I treated him after the river incident, this time for sure. He was just trying to be nice. Should I do the apology before or after the presentation? Maybe after. He looks kind of tensed up right now.

Okay, admit it, Bronte. You came just to see how he handles himself. And you've started thinking about him a lot, and looking out for him. Your heart beats faster when he comes to parkour. And sometimes you think he's watching you.

He's trouble, and the last thing you need is another Middle Eastern boyfriend. But Karam is different from Sarfraz. He doesn't have a hard edge. He's thoughtful, and he's trying hard to fit in and make friends. You could help him with that. Guys who smile stick around for a while. Oh, me and my lame rhymes.

Anyway, I'm here to support him. Sort of. Or maybe to make friends with Pearl, who's an intriguing mystery. Can I bring her out of her shell? Could I become a better person by hanging out with her instead of my cheerleader friends?

They can be so... juvenile. They didn't used to be, or maybe I was? Can I prove to Jazz and Nat she's okay? She is okay, right?

I turn to look at Pearl, chatting excitedly with her cousin. She's wearing a long black skirt under a tunic-style red shirt that comes almost to her knees. Her hijab is a silky beige worn over a black under-cap, and it has a thick black border along the edge that's draped in front of her left shoulder. It's fastened with bead-decorated pins woven through the layers of the hijab.

Where does she shop for hijabs in Richland, Washington? Where does she find the pretty pins that fasten them? How does she keep her headscarves from slipping? How did she know which day to start wearing one?

Stop, Bronte. Enough with the stupid questions. Just sit with your mouth zipped and watch. Hope that Karam comes to Natalie's party tonight. Tommy said he's going to. You'll wear something conservative, "modest" as my mom would say. My mom who's so into socializing with all her Richland friends again, and maybe so tired of butting heads with me, that she doesn't even bother asking me where or who I'm with half the time anymore. It feels like when we lost Dad, we lost my only parent.

The room is one-third full. Lots of young people from the mosque, it seems, with black, brown, and white faces, sitting in a tight knot and chatting excitedly like they know one another. The girls in the group are wearing hijabs. Did the imam order them to come support Karam, or are they here for the free food?

There's a nervous-looking plump couple Pearl is beaming at. I'm guessing they're her parents. There are also a few steely-faced middle-aged and elderly white couples.

"Building cultural bridges," reads a poster at the front. People are lined up to sign it. A local priest is second in line, chatting with parishioners behind him. I relax a little. In fact, there's also a minister from Richland Episcopal. I'm impressed.

Two young couples are dressed like they think this is the Sixties: the guys in beads and beards, the women in wraparound skirts and lace-up leather boots. Well away from them is a frowning guy wearing a flak jacket. Now two non-Islam kids from my high school enter. They barely nod at me —no one I know very well.

Sheriff Macdonald, the local top cop, strides in looking like he's taking inventory. Hmm. Does he expect trouble, or has he come to get educated? I also spot two white girls my age—sisters, I'm guessing from their similar looks. They go to a different high school, but I recognize them as working at a local fast-food joint.

They're whispering as one pages through a Quran, the holy book of Muslims, and the other holds a copy of *Islam for Dummies*. No hijabs hide their streaked blond and pink hair. They wear enough Goth makeup and nose, ear, and eyebrow rings to attract looks from the sheriff, and the tight black shirts they're wearing plunge way too low for my taste, let alone for a public seminar on Islam.

Whatever. Be happy for Pearl and Karam that anyone from good ol' Richland has shown.

A cough from Karam prompts people to stop chatting and sit up straight. He has moved to the podium, while Pearl sits in a chair behind him with head lowered and hands in her lap, as if hoping all attention will be directed to her cousin today. I notice a slim, thirtyish guy wearing a short, round, brimless cap and loose, ankle-length grey garment, slide into the chair beside the mosque bouncer—er, caretaker. Clearly, the imam. He looks totally friendly and approachable. Why should that surprise me?

"Good morning. I'm Karam Saif, and this is my cousin Pearl. We're originally from Yemen, which is in the Middle East, but we live here now and attend Three Rivers High School and the Richland Masjid, or Mosque. We'd like to extend a warm welcome to all of you. We are offering this morning's program to bridge cultures and correct any misinformation that might be out there."

He pauses as the rear door opens and shuts quietly. I turn to see Mr. Legendre slip in with an apologetic look on his face. He sits down beside the imam and mosque caretaker.

"So," Karam continues, "I'll begin with some basic information, and then Pearl and I will answer questions."

He pauses. It's quiet as a funeral parlour.

"Islam is the world's second-largest religion. It began in the early seventh century in Mecca, a city in Saudi Arabia, before spreading throughout the Middle East. It's defined by our holy book, the Quran, which we consider the final revelation of God—the same God worshipped by Jews and Christians—whom we call Allah. Allah is simply the Arabic word for 'God.' Islam, a word that means 'peace and submission to God,' was revealed through such prophets as Adam, Noah, Abraham, Moses, Jesus, and Muhummad—peace be upon him—Muhammad being the last prophet of God, in our belief. So naturally, we share many of the same beliefs as Christians and Jews."

"Not hardly!" the guy in the flak jacket shouts.

Karam ignores him. "We practise the five pillars of Islam, all acts of worship: faith, prayer, charity, fasting during Ramadan, and a pilgrimage to Mecca. We follow lessons and guidance from the Quran and hadith, which are the narrated accounts of our Prophet's (peace be upon him) words and actions during his lifetime. The Quran and hadith both promote peace, mercy, and respect for other religions. Islam also encourages us to do good deeds, like charity and kindness to others, while building our spiritual relationship with God." He coughs again. There's a glisten of sweat on his forehead.

Pearl's face is glowing with pride. So far, so good, I figure.

"Okay, questions from the audience?"

"Yeah, what's the difference between a Muslim and a Moslem and an Islamist?" asks a middle-aged Caucasian woman in designer glasses.

"Muslim isn't an English word," Karam says with a slight smile, "so it ends up getting pronounced different ways. Although a Muslim, Moslem, and Islamist are the same thing – people who practice Islam and submit to God – most Muslims call themselves 'Muslim,' pronounced with an S, not a Z. A Muslim practises Islam, like a Christian practises Christianity or a Jew practises Judaism."

Okay, at least I knew that much. The woman nods, apparently satisfied.

One of the hippie ladies stands up. "Why do women have to cover themselves?"

Pearl rises shyly, like they have been expecting this one and agreed she'd tackle it. "If a woman chooses to wear a hijab, or head scarf, it is out of modesty and a desire to please God, as he instructed us to do in the Quran. It also helps us show pride in our faith. We consider it a shield against degrading remarks and unwanted attention. In fact, it liberates us. By not putting our bodies on display, we are more likely to be judged by our intellect, social interactions, and inner spiritual beauty rather than by our superficial appearance."

"But women aren't even allowed to worship next to men!" the woman's companion protests in a loud voice.

"Men and women pray separately, because prayer is meant to be a distraction-free opportunity to connect with God. It's about modesty. Our worship is very physical: We stand, bow, and prostrate ourselves many times. This can be awkward if you're trying to be modest but you're next to someone of the other gender."

"Hadn't thought of that!" the woman minister says.

Hmm, new to me too. Nice going, Pearl! I wonder about visiting the masjid. Maybe doing a class there to learn more. Ha! I could do it just to freak out my mother. Or, I chide myself, I could do it to be more educated about the countries my dad is covering.

"Can Muslim teens date? Can they have boyfriends or girlfriends?" No way! Did I actually stand up and ask that? I don't seem to have control of my big mouth.

Pearl, who was about to sit down, twirls and smiles falteringly, while Karam stands there with a beet-red face. I feel three pairs of eyes on me: Mr. Legendre's, the imam's, and the caretaker's.

"Different Muslims follow different guidelines on that," Pearl says, "but in general, we avoid situations that might tempt couples from not abstaining till marriage."

Now it's my face burning up, as I plop back into my folding chair. Pearl Saif actually almost said the word "sex?" Well, how about that? ROTFL

A heavy, bald man stands and strokes his moustache, staring straight at Karam. "If Moslems are fighting to form an

Islamic State, how can you say your religion promotes peace?"

Karam stands tall and looks directly at the questioner. "An Islamic State is the idea of a nation-state founded on Islamic law and politics. Islam absolutely condemns violence, and nothing in our faith encourages suicide bombings or terrorism. The Quran places great value on human life. It says in Chapter Five that '... whoever kills a soul...it is as if he had slain mankind entirely. And whoever saves one life, it is as if he had saved mankind entirely.'"

"Not true!" shouts a voice from someone who has just entered the room.

Shit. Of course, it would be Dan.

"Islam encourages people to do terrible things. Like behead Christians! Why don't you go back where you came from?" He's waving his sign in some kind of triumphant manner, and he's pink in the face with excitement.

Could the guy be any more of a jerk? I watch Sheriff MacDonald rise, but he doesn't move forward, as if waiting to see what will happen.

"Good morning, Dan," Karam says in a pleasant, steady voice. "Yes, there are extremists who use the name of Islam to commit acts of terror. And often, those with little to no knowledge of Islam hold the faith responsible for the acts of a fringe minority among Muslims.

"The overwhelming majority of Muslims are as repulsed and horrified by acts of terrorism as you are. Also, the terrorists you're referring to target innocent Muslims far more than they do Christians or other sects.

"There are also people of other faiths who have been committing horrific acts in the name of their religion: Buddhist monks attacking Muslims in Burma, the Klu Klux

Klan Christians who are violent in the name of white supremacy. These groups' religions are never made to blame for a few people's actions... so why do all Muslims get the blame for a few random extremists?"

"Hear, hear," says the priest, and there's a smattering of clapping.

"I have a question for the imam," says a Hispanic parent of one of the Three Rivers High School students.

Karam looks at the imam, who nods and stands.

"Given the attempts Muslim extremists have been making at recruiting and radicalizing Western youth, what do you as leader of the local mosque do to monitor or prevent that kind of activity?"

"That is an excellent question, and obviously of grave concern to us. The answer is that as an imam, I am in a position to know and counsel members of my congregation, so I not only ensure they understand the true tenets of our faith, which forbid injustice and violence, but I also counsel anyone who appears to be starting on that path. Meanwhile, members of our mosque actively watch and listen for such signs. If I have suspicions and feel I cannot nip them in the bud, I communicate with local police and school staff.

"To that end, I have taken the time to build relationships with our local sheriff, school board members, teachers, other local religious leaders, and the community at large. This session, which by the way was young Karam's idea, is an example of the kind of bridging that can prevent and address the dangers of radicalization, as well as inform fellow townspeople."

The minister stands to clap vigorously. Soon, others rise to do the same, me too, until there's an all-out standing ovation and roar of approval.

Imam Taha seems to take that as encouragement to add, "Our congregation members who regularly attend prayers and participate in mosque activities are part of a community. They feel like they belong. I do everything within my means to keep that feeling of community and family alive among my members, because it prevents people from feeling lonely or like an outcast. People, Muslim or otherwise, join hate groups and gangs to gain a sense of belonging."

Karam and Pearl stand proud, perhaps also relieved, while the imam quietly takes his seat again. A sense of belonging, I reflect sadly. Something I've lost and don't know how to get back.

For the next half hour, Karam and Pearl take more questions, some polite, some naïve, some ridiculous or rude. They handle them like pro baseball players who never strike out or hit a foul ball. Despite all that, I don't really believe Karam is all that religious. Just a feeling I have. They said it was Karam's idea but probably Pearl or his imam put him up to this.

Though I'm pleased the thing is going well, I'm tired enough to be half nodding off by the time one of the fast-food girls rises and smiles over-wide at Karam.

"Such good answers, Karam." She pronounces the name almost flirtatiously, like she's about to ask him on a date. "So, how can people like us help the Moslems—er, Muslims—who are getting bombed over there?"

Karam is smooth. "Come talk to me afterwards," he says, checking his watch. "I believe we're out of time, but thanks to everyone for coming, and Pearl and I will be up here a while longer to chat with anyone who wishes."

He's looking at the fast-food sisters, not at me. Then he gets thronged by the buzzing crowd, the fast-foodies at the head of the pack, which kind of destroys my plan to go apologize to him and maybe draw him out for a cup of coffee. I can't even see Pearl anymore, the way her mosque crowd is surrounding her and speaking in excited voices.

I see Dan staring at me for a minute before he slinks out the back door, Sheriff MacDonald behind him. Welcome to Richland, Dan. Maybe you should go back to where *you* came from.

CHAPTER EIGHT

"You look nice," my mother says, like she's trying.

I'm at the living room window waiting for Tommy's dented green pickup truck to pull up. I've opted for not-tight jeans and a long-sleeved, high-necked blouse with bits of embroidery. Low-key and feminine, I'm hoping, but don't say it to Mom.

"Thanks."

"Enjoy your party and say hi to Natalie's parents for me."

Ha, little does she know (or really care?) the parents are out of town.

"I will," I lie as Tommy pulls into the driveway. I dash out and leap in the front seat.

"Hey, Bronte," he says. "You know I'm picking up Karam too, right?"

"Yup," I say, heart fluttering.

He pulls up to Pearl's house and lays on the horn. "Tommy! You have to go to the door!" I urge.

Pearl's hefty-sized father shuffles out onto the front steps with a frown.

"This is how you call on Karam?" he addresses Tommy as the two of us approach a little sheepishly.

Pearl's mother appears behind him, draped in black from head to toe, vaguely reminding me of a nun. I decide her face is kind-looking, even if she's pursing her lips about the horn honking.

"Um, sorry, Mr. Saif," Tommy says as I all but hide behind him.

"Hi Tommy and Bronte," Karam says as he appears, looking pretty hot in new jeans and a blue button-up shirt. "Uncle Lando, Aunt Reem, this is Tommy and Bronte."

"Nice to meet you," they say a little stiffly. Then Uncle Lando turns to Karam. "Be home by eleven, and do nothing to disgrace yourself or our family."

"Don't worry, Uncle Lando," Karam says fondly.

The couple nods at us, back away, and disappear inside.

"Hi Tommy, hi Bronte," comes Pearl's voice as she appears in the doorway, a rather serious expression on her face, bits of hair escaping from a navy hijab. "Be careful, Karam."

"Of what?" he asks with a hint of annoyance. "And why won't you go too?"

"Drugs, alcohol, and—" She stops. "People look to us as examples of—"

"I'm trying to make friends," Karam says, "not be Mr. Perfect. This is America, not Yemen."

She turns aside and looks away, like he has struck her.

"I'm sorry, Pearl," he says, lowering his head.

But she's so far back down the hallway by then, she probably doesn't hear him. Karam closes the front door softly on quiet Middle Eastern music coming from an old-school stereo.

Minutes later, we're in the car, Tommy at the wheel, careening around corners on our way to a hilly suburb the other side of town.

"This is going to be wicked fun," Tommy says.

"What does wicked fun mean?" Karam asks, frowning.

Feeling a little tongue-tied, I shrug like I'm not on translator duty tonight. Tommy smiles and looks over his shoulder at Karam. "This party is at Natalie's place. Her folks are both lawyers, and they're made of money."

We approach her lit-up house the size of a mansion. As we exit the truck, I can feel the ground throbbing with pop music. There's laughter and splashes from the rear. Karam's eyes go a little wide.

Tommy steers us through a side gate towards the racket. I notice Karam's jaw loosen to see a swimming pool lit up both under the water and from above. There are two inflatable crocodiles floating in it. Ryker is actually riding one, dressed only in swimming trunks.

"Hey there, Kazam, Tommy, Bronte!" Ryker calls out while making a feeble attempt to do a handstand on his ride. Giggling girls take photos with their cell phones. "Join me?"

"You must be joking. It's freezing!" Karam says.

"Freezing? It's a balmy fifty degrees Fahrenheit!"

"Thanks, but we'll just watch," I say, amused.

The pool is surrounded by padded deck chairs filled with Three Rivers High School students holding drinks. Lots more people are hanging around inside the house.

"Where are the parents and why would they allow this?" Karam whispers to me, still clutching a can of fizzy orange juice he brought from home.

"This is America," I whisper back. "They're away, trusting their daughter not to have a party."

Tommy hands a twelve-pack to a guy. Karam offers up his orange juice like a question mark and someone grabs it from hands.

"The drinks we bring are our entrance fee?" Karam asks Tommy.

"Basically, yes," he says, laughing. "But it doesn't mean you have to drink alcohol."

Someone pops a top off a brown bottle and shoves it into my hands, then Karam's. Having lost his O.J., he holds it like a prop without actually drinking from it. I take a deep swig and wave to Jazel, who's dancing with some other cheerleaders, wearing a yellow top that doesn't quite meet up with the waistband of her camo pants.

Karam's phone buzzes.

I eye him as he seizes it from his pocket and moves away with long strides. Standing beside a flag pole, he studies the message, frowning, then catches me watching him and turns further away. I see him shaking his head, punching in a reply, and giving the pole a hard kick before he repockets the phone.

"Something wrong?" I ask as he returns.

"No," he says, jaw so tight it looks like it's going to break.

"There must be fifty people here," Tommy says.

"Mmm, both boys and girls," Karam observes, like a mixed party is a wonder. Gazing at everyone through Karam's eyes, I note they're dressed in crazy, tight clothing. And some couples are dancing together!

"What are you thinking?" I ask, leaning in a little.

"That the pirated Hollywood movies my friends and I used to download weren't fantasy. Life here really is about pool parties? If it were summer, would the girls be in bikinis?"

"Yes, and that would freak you out," I sympathize. "There's only so much new culture a guy can take just two months in. Alexandria was a big-time adjustment for me."

He gazes at me shyly, appreciatively, and says in Arabic, "I'm sure it was, but Egypt is a lot more liberal than Yemen." Then he lifts his head and trails after Tommy, like he's determined to prove he does this kind of party all the time. Karam, the newly-minted all-American guy.

"Karam, Tommy, Bronte, so glad you made it!" Natalie greets us, sashaying up in baby-blue designer boots, her heavily made-up eyes darting around. She uses her phone to snap pictures of us as I look over her clingy tank, colorful leggings, and expensive footwear. She has definitely spent time with her hair curler and makeup tonight, I reflect with amusement as she blinks at us in her glued-on fake eyelashes. She wasn't that into fashion when we started hanging out two years ago, but hey, people change, I remind myself. Karam startles for a second as Natalie takes his hand and leads him to a table heavy with food.

"Try one of my amazing brownies?"

Just as Karam's about to take one to be polite, I step between him and the plate.

"Natalie, it's Karam's first Richland party. Tommy and I are his chaperones, and I know what's in those brownies," I tease her. "Karam, stick to the hummus and crackers, or Pearl will kill us."

Natalie erupts into hyena-like giggles. Karam looks mystified but steps away from the table.

"Karam! You were awesome today! Didn't know you'd be here," says one of the two girls who were at the seminar earlier. She and her sister are wearing skin-tight leggings, high heels, and see-through tops.

"Hi," he says, glancing around nervously like he's trying not to stare at them. I step back with narrowed eyes.

"Ha! So you know people here who aren't even from Three Rivers High School," Tommy accuses Karam as he gulps beer, eyeing the pair with interest. "Aren't you going to introduce me?"

"Um, sure. This is Chloe and Caitlin. Girls, this is my friend Tommy."

The girls crowd in so tightly that it's a good fifteen minutes before Karam finds me again, with Jazel at the edge of the room.

"There you are." His face is tense and his forehead reveals a line of sweat. Is he into them? "How are you doing?" he asks, gripping his beer bottle with white knuckles.

"Great," I say, allowing a hint of chill in my voice. "You escaping your groupies?"

He shakes his head, frowning. "What are groupies, Bronte?"

I say the word in Arabic, and he laughs. My tensed shoulders relax.

He's staring at my hair, then raises a finger like he's about to touch it, but doesn't.

"What?" I tease, tossing my head.

"Your hair is like gold," he says.

My chest tingles. "Wow, nicest compliment I've had all evening." There's a second of awkward silence. I feel myself sweating like at the seminar. "You did well today, Karam. Sorry you got sort of heckled at times." I lift my beer to my lips and take a swallow to calm my nerves.

"Thanks. The imam prepared us well. I'm just glad it's over. I appreciate your coming."

"No problem. You drinking that?" I raise an eyebrow and point to his beer.

"Yeah. I mean, um, no."

I smile. "Your choice. Doesn't bother me either way."

"Hey, your dimples come out when you smile," he says. His hand rises slowly towards them. Then, daringly, he touches one, ever so gently, with a fingertip.

The electrical surge through my body is enough to trigger a neighbourhood power outage. To my astonishment, I find myself leaning in and kissing him, full on the lips.

When we finally pull away, his eyes are sparkling, and his trembling hand dares to linger on mine.

"I've been meaning to apologize," I say softly, enjoying the new color in his cheeks.

"For what?"

"The way I acted after the river rescue. I didn't thank you. I was too—too embarrassed."

"No worries," he says, a phrase he must have picked up from Tommy. He leans in close again and looks me in the eyes, like he's working up the nerve to initiate the kiss this time.

I don't move away, but the moment is interrupted by a commotion behind us.

"Hey, Parkour Club!" It's Ryker, still in swimming trunks, droplets flying as he tosses his long wet hair over his shoulders and yanks a staggering Dan—when did he arrive? —to the diving board. "Let's do us a show!"

He leaps up onto the diving board, springing off it side-ways and landing in the water with his hands curled around the edge of the pool. One quick lift and he's galloping play-fully on all fours across the tiles of the pool deck. Dan makes a fool of himself trying to follow Ryker, hobbling after him in an awkward running squat, missing the rhythm. Karam and I chuckle.

"Eyyyiii!" comes a shriek. It's Natalie, hanging precariously out a second-floor window of the house. "Come on, Jazz, Bronte, Tommy, Karam. Let's show 'em what we can do!"

Her words are a little slurred. I rush to the garden plot below her window in case she falls, but she manages the drop from second- to ground-floor windowsill in her new boots, catching an adjacent shutter with her hands, then bouncing down to the ground. Hands firmly on my shoulder, she pulls me into the line-up of traceurs and traceuses strutting around the pool like some cheap chorus-line show. Karam grins and joins in. Next thing I know, we've all broken apart to demonstrate gymnastic tricks. A pretty sloppy demo, in my opinion, but it's definitely fun being part of a group firing up the crowd.

I throw a look at Karam, who grins and amps up the energy of his moves. The rest of the partygoers are clapping in time. "Ryker! Ryker!" they're saying, because he's in the lead.

Faster and faster we go, throwing all sorts of flip variations off the house walls, pool loungers, and drain pipes outside, then the chairs and sofas and kitchen counters inside, all to screams of approval.

"Finale!" shouts Ryker, as we circle back to the pool deck. He runs at a shed ten feet behind the pool's deep end, then jumps up, stepping against the side of it and springing to its roof. He throws in a side flip while accelerating across the roof ridge, then takes a flying leap across an expanse of partygoers with necks craned, and lands with a major splash in the pool.

There's whistling and clapping and then a rush of eager hands to pull him out.

"More whiskey," he moans as he lies full length on the tiles beside the pool with a silly grin. Someone hands him a towel.

"More whiskey for Ryker!" Dan shouts.

"Sorry, guys, we're outta whiskey," Natalie informs them with a dramatic sigh.

"That, madam, can be changed!" Dan announces, leaping up and bowing. "Ryker and I will find more. Won't we?"

"At your service, Natalie," Ryker says, struggling up, detouring inside to change into his dry street clothes, and following Dan through the swinging side gate.

"Hope they're not driving," I say to no one in particular.

"I think they don't need more whiskey," Karam suggests. I watch him lift his beer to his lips and take a tiny sip.

"Eeuw! Can't believe I just did that!" he says, wiping his mouth in disgust, setting the bottle down, and moving away from it.

I'm nearly keeled over with laughter as I grab his hand and say, "Want to lose this place?"

"Pardon?" he asks, running a hand through his hair.

"Let's go for a walk," I say in Arabic.

"Okay," he says in a pleased voice.

We tell Tommy, who raises his eyebrow and gives us a thumb's-up. Sign language Karam doesn't need interpreted into English or Arabic.

We begin by jogging through the lamp-lit streets, swinging around the occasional sign post, and konging— leapfrogging—over a dumpster. Then we ramp it up to progressively bigger vaults and running jumps wherever we see them, and pretty soon it's clear we're trying to outdo each other in a friendly way.

The cool night air kisses my warming face as we move through the landscape together. Happiness chases away the shadows in my soul. We bound past big houses decorated with Halloween skeletons and carved pumpkins, and play-fully try to clear wide driveways lit up by expensive-looking orange twinkle-lights, then race into the downtown core. Past hardware stores, manicure parlours, and all-night grocery stores. Lots of cars and trucks pass us, some honking in applause or irritation at our antics. We don't care.

He cups his hands in front of my waist, and I lift my right foot and slot it there to perform a flip, which I follow up with a beautiful slide-vault over a low wall, landing silently on the other side.

We're breathing hard now, exhilarated, when Karam halts and holds up his hand.

"What?" I whisper, coming close, tingling with happi-ness at breathing in his scent and having his face just inches from mine.

"See those lights?" he asks.

"Two flashlights moving around. So?"

"That's a liquor store. See the sign that says 'Closed for renovations'? Someone's checking the place out."

"You mean casing it." I take a few steps forward, watch for a minute, then pull out my phone and punch in 9-1-1.

"What are you doing?"

"Calling police. Hello? Yes, robbery in progress." I name the nearest cross streets.

"I don't think they'll get here in time," Karam says, pointing to two shadows that start climbing, somewhat falter-ingly, the nearest wall of the store.

"Why are they going up the wall?" Karam wonders. "Maybe they think they can break in through the roof?"

I freeze. "Whoever they are, they know parkour." The shadows are ascending the building using well-placed wall-run steps, and they mount its wall from a hanging position called a climb-up.

"Yes? Well, so do we," Karam declares.

I grab his elbow to stop him, but he shakes me off and approaches the store soundlessly. I watch him leap onto a bench and stride upwards, catching the edge of the flat tar roof and quickly mounting it, just as a large bubble of glass— a rooftop skylight—shatters a few feet away. The silhouette of a young man with long hair and a raised axe turns just long enough to see Karam, then hurls itself over the far side of the building, following another moving shadow.

It would have been effortless for Karam to descend with them, match their every move, and capture them for police. But he turns when I scream, "No, Karam! They might be armed!"

He descends and runs back to me. Sensing I'm panicked and fearful for both of us, he wraps his arms around me.

But thick, muscular arms tear him off me. And others pull me away from him.

"No!" I shout as the cops put a chokehold on Karam, twist his hands behind his back, then clamp something onto his wrists.

"Young lady, are you okay? You, boy, are under arrest for breaking and entering, and trying to assault this girl. And since I smell alcohol on your breath, we'll be Breathalysing you too."

CHAPTER NINE

"I don't care if it's the school counsellor, some private shrink she recommends, or the minister at the church we used to go to!" Mom is shouting. "You need help, Bronte."

"I don't need help! And I don't need you yelling at me!"

Mom lowers her voice, but her words still hit me like acid.

"What do you think it feels like to have my daughter brought home in a patrol car, because some boy she's carousing with has been arrested for breaking into a liquor store? You were supposed to be at Natalie's house."

"He wasn't arrested. He was detained till they realized he was—"

"I don't care about that. I care about you, Bronte." Her voice goes quieter. "Wandering around in the worst part of downtown with a boy you hardly know is a sign you need help. Not to mention your behaviour with me at home, your dropping grades, and how you seem depressed half the time. Wouldn't you agree? Do I need to ground you, or will you agree to speak with someone?"

So she actually cares? Her eyes are moist. She tries to put her hand on my shoulder and draw me close. A part of me wants to melt into her, wants to cry a sea of tears. If she were Dad, I would do exactly that. But I'm more inclined to beat on her chest and tell her to turn back time and bring Dad home.

She's right that home stresses me out these days and I'm not concentrating well at school. I'm still an insomniac suffering from nightmares about Dad, and of course I'm sad he's not here.

"I'm fine. I just need fresh air," I declare, stalking past her to the front door, grabbing my coat.

"I'll pay for whatever counsellor you choose," Mom calls after me, her voice sounding kind of desperate.

I don't answer, because I don't know what to say. Snow swirls around me. I walk faster to get warm, and wind my red wool scarf around my head and neck. I punch in Jazel's number on my phone.

"Hey, Bronte. How are you?"

"Not so great. Just had a fight with my mom. Can I come over?"

There's hesitation. She hasn't said much to me since I walked out of Natalie's party with Karam. Nor has Natalie, for that matter. What, they're not into me spending time with Karam? They feel sorry for me about Dad? They think I've changed, maybe see that I don't fit in here anymore? Aren't best friends supposed to stick with you through whatever? Have we grown so far apart we're not friends anymore?

"Can't right now," she says flatly. "I'm meeting someone in a few minutes. A date."

"Oh. Sorry. Do I get to know who?" I ask in what I hope is a light-hearted, teasing voice.

"Dan." Her tone has a barb in it.

Great. The bigoted would-be liquor-store burglar that Karam and I almost got arrested, if it was him and Ryker. No wonder she has been avoiding me.

"Cool," I say, maybe a little too coolly.

"Bronte," she says, voice lowered to almost a whisper.

"Yeah?"

"Are you seeing Karam? Like, are you guys an item?"

"No," I blurt out. But Jazz is, or was, my best friend. So I add, "Maybe. Wouldn't mind."

Again, a moment of silence. Then, "Careful, Bronte."

I grit my teeth but don't feel like having an all-out phone fight with Jazel, who's being fed who knows what kind of Islamaphobic drivel by her new Texan babe.

"Later," I say, feeling suddenly tired enough to lie down on the snow-powdered park bench beside me and sleep.

"Later," she says, but she sounds so far away.

I trudge forward, watching the imprints my feet make in the snow. I stare blandly at a trellis wall with dead vines, and the chipped brick steps leading up to a park gazebo. I'm too chilled and distracted to use any of these features for parkour moves, like I usually do.

My mom's stinging words run through my head. The minister at the church we used to go to? That'd be a joke. No one in our family has been to church in five years. My parents kind of lost their church-going habits when Dad started chasing around war zones. School counsellor? What would she know? And someone would see me go into that office and start rumours.

But it's true I'm a little out of whack these days. I just need to get away from our toxic house sometimes. Like this walk by myself in the frigid air. More importantly, I need to find out if Karam's okay. Did his aunt and uncle believe him? I mean, the cops never caught the two guys who really were trying to break in, and we never got a good enough look to say for sure if they were Ryker and Dan. Which is probably a good thing. Would I turn in my fellow traceurs? Probably not.

It was all bad timing, bad luck, a bad night. The least I can do is—

I stop when I find myself in front of Pearl's house. Almost like I'd planned to end up here. I've never been inside her place, of course. But maybe I can explain about the other night to his family, or at least to Pearl, and make sure he's not in deep shit. The worst they can do is slam the door in my face, right? But I imagine Pearl's parents being really nice, a happy family, calm people who pray five times a day and love each other. Not like mine.

Just like last time, warm light and Arab music leak out of the bay window of their simple one-storey, making me nostalgic for Egypt. There's a moment's silence after I ring the doorbell. Then Uncle Reem opens the door.

"Oh," he says on finding a shivering girl standing on the front steps, head wrapped in a red wool scarf.

"I'm, um, Bronte. We met once before. Is Pearl home?" I ask in Arabic, suddenly shy.

Aunt Reem bustles towards me, her fingers hastily adjusting a blue hijab.

"Come in, dear, out of the cold!" she urges in Arabic. "Pearl! Pearl! You have a visitor! I've just made some karak and masoob, Bronte. Would you like some?"

Karak is a spicy milk tea, and masoob a delicious banana dish with cream, cheese, dates, and honey. "For sure. Thank you," I say.

The welcoming scent wafts through the air, as does the soft Arab music. I step across the doorsill and shed my coat and boots, but not my scarf.

The tiny living room is overpowered by multilayered swag velvet curtains with dangling tassels in purple and gold, sort of Arabian Nights-style. There are enough coordinating pillows to support a major-league pillow fight.

"Bronte!" Pearl's eyebrows are raised, but she offers a beaming smile. Her thick black hair hangs loose about her shoulders. It's totally weird to see her hair and neck. "What a surprise. Yes, come in. Karam is at the library doing homework."

Phew. Not sure if I could face him in front of his entire family.

"I came to, um, tell you what happened the other night," I say once I'm seated and sipping the steaming cup of tea, which is sweetly calming. I spoon some of the banana dish into my mouth, and let its delicious, familiar flavour light up my taste buds and memories of Egypt.

They study me carefully, all ears.

"We were just going for a walk when we saw a robbery in progress. I called the police, but Karam thought he should try to stop them, in case the police didn't arrive in time."

The aunt is nodding. The uncle sits in a big brown easy chair, his face alert but eyes averted from me.

"I got scared they might hurt us and started shouting. Karam would have chased and caught them, but he came back to see if I was okay. The police initially thought he was one of the robbers but understood when we explained things. Karam didn't do anything wrong. He was brave and thoughtful. You should be proud of him," I finish.

"But he drank liquor at this party, yes?" the uncle asks in a deep voice.

"He took one sip, and then he was all mad he'd even done that. I know that for absolute sure."

Pearl's father is frowning and looking at his wife. Pearl is studying the table.

"Thank you, Bronte, for taking the trouble to come and talk with us," Karam's uncle finally says.

"You're welcome." I feel tension drain from the air.

"You're the girl who lived in Egypt for a while?" the aunt asks me.

"I am."

I tell them the nice parts about living in Alexandria. They tell me about coming from Yemen many years ago. I get to eat some more Middle Eastern treats I haven't seen or smelled since I used to check out the bakeries in Egypt. They listen to me talk about my dad's career, and furrow their eyebrows when they hear he's in Yemen.

"I've always dreamed of visiting Egypt one day," Pearl reveals shyly.

"It will never happen, since we don't play the lottery," her father teases her.

When conversation lags, Pearl asks, "Want to hang out in my room?"

"Sure," I say, tired out by my efforts in Arabic and happy to escape the parents.

Her room is small but super tidy, with pastel green walls, a poster of a cat, Islamic calligraphy art, and a beautiful red rug on one wall that makes me think of Aladdin's flying carpet.

"Father was not pleased with Karam, but it is mostly smoothed over now. Especially with you coming to explain, I think." She smiles at me, then points to my wool scarf and giggles. "You can take that off now."

I grin and tug it off.

"Want to practise your Arabic some more?"

"Actually, I think I'm exhausted after talking with your parents," I say, adding, "but they're very nice."

"They are," she agrees.

"How is Karam dealing with having lost his family?" It's a big question, but when and who else would I ever ask?

She studies her fingernails, which are polished a rose pink. "It has been rough on him, but we don't really talk about it. I can't even imagine." She's quiet for a minute, then offers a smile. "He's such a positive person, and so determined to fit in. That helps. He's sure making friends quickly."

She looks at me like the last bit is a question, but I don't bite.

"And you? How are you?" Pearl asks, her large brown eyes earnest.

"I'm a mess." I half laugh, but she doesn't laugh back. "My dad being in Yemen, that's scary. My mom and I don't get along, so I don't spend much time at home. And I think my mom and dad are breaking up."

"Whoa, that's a major load of nasty stuff to deal with," Pearl says. "If you need someone to talk to, I'm not a bad listener." She leans forward awkwardly to hug me.

I start blabbering on about everything from my mom's and my fights to worrying about Dad and missing Sarfraz. Tears slide down my cheeks as her arms wrap around me. I'm blubbering like a baby on poor Pearl's sweater. Pearl, who I hardly even know.

"Have you talked to anyone about this besides me?" she asks quietly.

"No. And I'm sorry I'm being such a wreck in front of you. I'm never like this, you know. It's just that you're so, well, chill. Even when kids give you shit at school. Can you, like, sell me a little of your calm cologne or whatever it is that makes you so—?"

She's smiling now, and I'm smiling through my tears.

"I'm not always calm," she protests. "But maybe my faith helps. Anyway, there's a school counsellor, you know."

"Not her," I say, making a face.

Pearl grins. "Mmm. She is kind of a sad sack, isn't she? Do you have a religious leader? Do you go to church?"

I shake my head. "What about your imam? Does he counsel teenagers who are kind of falling apart?" I grin to show I'm kidding.

Pearl takes a deep breath and doesn't treat it as a joke. "There are lots of former refugees at our masjid—teens and adults—that Imam Taha has had to help with trauma."

"Yeah, I suppose. Pearl, I was thinking. Could I maybe come to your mosque with you sometime? Just to see it. I mean, if you're allowed visitors. I'd have to learn how to wear a hijab."

"That's for sure," she teases. "Is this about Karam, Bronte?"

"No! Not at all. I'm just curious, you know?"

She presses her lips flat and studies my face closely. "Okay. We welcome visitors sincere in wanting to know more about our faith. The Richland mosque is small and plain on the outside, but the congregation is growing. We have almost fifty brothers and sisters coming regularly now. People who've moved to Richland from India, Pakistan,

Syria, Indonesia, everywhere. Imam Taha and the women's board allow me to plan activities for the young sisters. I've started an exercise class, seminars on health, and an Islam education circle."

Her face is animated, her long eyelashes blinking rapidly.

"That's great," I say.

"There's a group of boys that plays volleyball, soccer, and foosball every Wednesday night. I haven't talked Karam into joining them yet. And there are study sessions for new Muslims on Saturdays."

"One step at a time," I say, grabbing a tissue from the box on her dresser and blowing my nose. I look at myself in her mirror. "Arggh. I'm a mess."

"Nothing that can't be fixed. Want me to give you a makeover? I love putting makeup on my friends. I do a mean manicure too. Might study to be a makeup artist when I finish school."

"Seriously? I thought maybe you'd take over your father's jewellery store, given your name."

She laughs softly. "Who knows? What about you?"

"I want to run a parkour gym for kids."

"I've heard that. Sounds perfect for you. Now, here's some makeup remover, then wash your face in the bathroom down the hall, and we'll start."

"Hey, I'm excited. And after the makeover, can I try on some of your hijabs?" I lift a pink and yellow silk one off a rack on her dresser.

"Get your hands off! You're not wearing my favourite one!" she protests, giggling.

So my first rockin' evening in a long time begins. We do selfies after some hijab fittings, and I post them on my social media. Ten minutes later, I think better of it and press delete.

The fun lasts till I leave and am walking home past the library. That's when I see Karam through the window, sitting super close to both the fast-food girls, sharing a laugh.

I grit my teeth, and not from the cold. Homework? Not effing likely. They don't even go to our school. I hustle past and peek back at them from another window. Karam is pointing to his computer screen, talking, and they're leaning in, faces lit up with excitement. No one else is in the library except the librarian and some guy in a black hoodie at a carousel on the opposite end, bent over his laptop.

I get a crazy impulse to hide in some trees across from the library entrance and wait for him. When he finally comes out, without the girls, I start tailing him like some delusional movie detective, for no good reason. When his phone buzzes, I move closer to listen in. I don't catch all of what he says, but the words "terrorist network" stop me dead. *I heard that wrong*, I tell myself. Totally, totally imagined it. Or he's talking about some news item. I had no right to follow him in the first place.

Karam doesn't see me turn and hurry home. I tell my mom a school friend has referred me to a counsellor and that he doesn't cost money.

She's so pleased she doesn't ask questions. I dive into bed numb and bewildered.

CHAPTER TEN

THREE WEEKS LATER, I OPEN THE BIG, HEAVY MOSQUE door and remove my shoes, the whole routine now a familiar habit.

"Bronte, *Assalamu alaikum wa rahmatullah*" [Peace be upon you and Allah's mercy], Imam Taha says with fondness in his deep voice, his hands in his robe pockets. He has kind eyes, that round white cap perched on his head I've learned is called a *kufi*, and a long grey cotton robe, a thobe, under whose hem small, bare feet poke out.

Once we are seated and he has poured me a cup of chai, his eyes are searching mine, like he can read my thoughts.

"*Assalamu alaikum*" [Peace be upon you], I say, eyeing the nearby plate of chocolate chip cookies.

"*Walaykum assalam wa rahmatullah wa brakatuh*" [And on you too be peace, and Allah's mercy and His blessings], he replies. "So now that we've been meeting for a few weeks, tell me overall how you're doing."

I smile at the imam, who I've really gotten to like—he's totally chill for a religious leader—while contemplating my answer. As usual, I ignore Mr. Noori, the scowling caretaker who sits in on our sessions because of some dumb mosque rule that the imam can't meet one-on-one with a female. Ha! Like I'm going to hit on Taha, or he's going to come on to me? But whatever. I understand, and Noori, who I secretly call Scarface for the ugly slash on one cheek, never says a word. Still, I don't like that he knows all my secrets now. Noori's dark eyes scan me from head to toe in a less-than-friendly fashion, as usual. His size and hardened face make my skin clammy—but that's a stupid way to think of a mosque care-taker, I tell myself.

"I'm, like, way better, Imam Taha. I don't worry about Dad all the time, I don't think about Sarfraz much anymore, and I'm finally sleeping okay, which means things are better with school and parkour. And I've been enjoying hanging with Pearl."

I tuck a stray strand of hair back under my hijab, which I wear only in the mosque, not at school or on dates with Karam. My mom has never seen one on me, on account of maybe it'd start a fight. Nor has she asked to meet Karam yet, maybe so we don't rock the boat on her and my slightly improved relationship.

"That's good, Bronte. I'm pleased for you. And you attribute this in part to the prayers and study circles you've been attending here?"

"Totally. Makes me so calm and peaceful—really." Strangely, instead of using it to rile up my mother, I've kept it secret from her so far.

"You've come a long way, Bronte. You're keeping physi-cally, mentally, and spiritually fit, for which I admire you. And how are things with your mother?"

He sits back in that ankle-length grey robe and cool *kufi*

of his, and steeples his long fingers together. Wonder what he'd do if I jumped up and hugged him for all the help he has given me? As if I would. It'd freak the poor guy out.

"Things are a little better with my mom. You're right that I had to try harder. I still get mad sometimes, but Dad's phoning more these days, which is good for all of us."

"Excellent. Is there anything else you'd like to say, Bronte?"

I dare myself to say it, and I do. "I'm in love, Imam Taha. Can't believe I'm telling you that, but that has really helped too."

He smiles warmly and twists the shiny gold wedding band on his finger. At least imams can marry, not like Catholic priests. And Pearl says he's a newlywed, so I figured maybe I could share that info.

"Love is a gift from Allah, Bronte. Accept it graciously and guard it well."

"For sure." Can't believe I'm blushing. "Oh! I almost forgot one other thing."

"Yes?"

"I've been getting some weird social-media comments from someone I don't know. They started after I posted a photo of myself in a hijab. A photo I took down ten minutes later."

He frowns. "Go on."

"He has to be local, 'cause he seems to know things about me. And I've blocked him, but he knows how to get around that. He's, like, encouraging me to explore Islam, and it's nothing more than that, but I don't like it."

"You obviously accepted his request to communicate with you in the first place. Are you replying to him?"

"Not yet. I mean, no."

"Good. Be careful, Bronte. I could have Mr. Noori here check it out. He's our I.T. guy."

I turn to look at Mr. Noori with a sliver of new respect.

"I could put blocks on all the software on your computer or try to track down the sender," Scarface Noori says, breaking his silence up till now in our sessions.

I hesitate. He's looking way too eagerly at the computer bag on my lap. "How about I just ignore them for now?" I say to the two men. "Or there's Mr. Legendre at school. The computer science teacher."

"Mr. Legendre is a good man," Imam Taha says. "Another option is Sheriff MacDonald, if the messages become in any way threatening."

"Yeah. Okay, Imam Taha. Thanks."

He rises but doesn't shake my hand, because I'm a girl—another Islamic tradition I've figured out—or walk me to the lobby. Unlike Scarface, who follows me right to the front door and watches me put on my shoes.

"Bronte, if you change your mind, I do know my way around computers."

"Okay, I'll keep that in mind." Maybe he's okay after all. His voice is way friendlier than his face.

"Also, I wanted to speak to you about the possibility of your becoming more involved with the sisters. You could help Pearl, or work with the younger children. Maybe we could schedule a time to talk about—"

"Thanks, Mr. Noori, but I'm not interested—I mean I'm not ready for all that. Take care." And I bolt out the mosque doors, slamming right into Sheriff Macdonald just as I'm yanking off my hijab.

"Sorry, Sheriff!"

"No problem, Bronte. How are you?"

I haven't seen him since the night Karam and I got shoved into a police cruiser and taken to police headquarters. There, he basically interrogated me about what I saw at the closed-down liquor store. But I don't want to think about that right now. Gotta get to parkour.

"I'm doing really well, Sheriff," I tell him truthfully.

"That's good, very good, Bronte," he says, patting my shoulder like I'm a pet dog. "Good to see you. Stay well." He says nothing about the hijab scrunched up in my hand, just disappears into the mosque, probably for more "let's work-together-for-our-community" plotting with Imam Taha.

"Karam!" I say, surprised and pleased to see him standing nearby, clearly waiting for me. "What's up?"

We hug and kiss, pretty daring given where we are. I know from my time in Egypt that Muslims usually don't date. There are ways to get to know people of the opposite sex, but it's generally through family activities, and carefully supervised. So I'm well aware that it's both daring and a little uncomfortable for Karam to be dating me. Three whole weeks so far! Then again, thanks to his enthusiasm to be American, he's maybe more proud of it than uncomfortable.

Karam reaches for my hand. Hopefully Noori's getting his thrills peeking out the window.

"Thought I'd walk you to parkour."

"Permission granted," I say, kissing him again. How lucky am I to have Karam in my life! It's like everything has turned around since we got together. Like my body is floating a foot off the ground every day. Even when it's cloudy, it feels gloriously sunny out. Life is good. So good, for once.

"How was your session?"

"Excellent, except for Scarface hanging around. I think I probably don't need to go anymore."

He squeezes my hand like he's proud of me. I wonder about bringing up the weird email thing, which I haven't told him about yet, but decide not to spoil the moment.

"So, we're going to totally whoop everyone at parkour today?" I tease.

"We'll never whoop Vansh. He has been working on that unreal polecat whenever Legendre isn't looking." A polecat is a jump into a hanging landing against a pole.

"Yeah, he thinks it'll land him in Hollywood," I say.

"More likely to land him in the hospital. It's so easy to miss your feet and slam against the pole!"

"Maybe. But I plan to try it sometime."

"You're the only girl I know who has a chance of getting it." He wraps me in his arms and gives me a wet kiss that sends delicious warmth through my body.

I pull away. "What's with those sisters who were all over you at Natalie's party? Chloe and Caitlin." I keep my tone casual, proud that I actually remember their names.

A shadow passes over his face. "At the party? I escaped them to find you, Bronte. Why would you care about them? They're just girls who tried to talk to me at Natalie's."

"And after your Islam talk. And at the library the other night, Karam."

His widened eyes scan my face. Long seconds pass before he speaks. "Okay, yes, I ran into them in the library. They asked me to recommend websites about Islam. But I'm not into them, Bronte. How could I be into anyone else, when I've got you?"

There's pleading in his voice, and the hands that grasp me around my waist are gentle, loving, and convincing. I'm still curious, but I let it drop, for now.

"Sorry, Karam. I just had to ask. You're everything that's

good in my life, and I couldn't handle losing you." I nuzzle his neck.

He spins me around so we're face to face. "Bronte, I'm not good with words, but you know what you mean to me, right? You rescued me from a dark place and helped me face forward again. I lost my family, my country, everything. You're all I've got. You have no reason to be jealous, ever."

I nod, guilt pricking me for even thinking of challenging him. I hold him tight. He all but clings to me in return. We've both been stressed. Maybe that's why we're drawn to each other. Maybe it's why we understand each other and were meant to be together. We're two birds, each with a broken wing. As one, we can fly. Sometimes I forget how much more he has suffered, because he doesn't show it. He's my inspiration that way.

"Karam?"

"Yes, Bronte." The warmth in his voice is welcome on this cool day.

"I should tell you why I needed to talk to Imam Taha."

"Okay." He leads me to a park bench, and we sit.

I spill everything: about the loneliness of trying to adapt to life in Egypt a year ago, about my mom forcing us to move home, my dad and mom being unofficially separated, my nightmares about Dad getting killed in Yemen, even about Sarfraz. He never interrupts, not once. He just holds me, strokes my hair.

"I'm so much better now," I finish.

"That's good."

"So, no secrets between us," I say.

He kisses my forehead by way of an answer.

I sob a little against his shoulder when I talk about my dad being in Yemen, and maybe never coming home. Pulling back a little, I look into his eyes. "Imam Taha says stress can put a person out of whack. He's a good guy, your imam. Have you talked to him much?"

"Not really. I'm actually not that religious. Theoretically our family was Muslim, but like many, my parents attended mosque services only once or twice a year, and didn't drop to their hands and knees to pray five times a day."

"You're not very religious but it was your idea to hold a seminar on Islam?" My suspiciousness bubbles to the surface again. Must find a way to ban these moments I don't trust Karam!

"Um, actually not my idea, but I was okay with it. Anyway, I agree that Imam Taha is a good guy. I'm glad he has helped you. And that you felt you could tell me—"

Bzzzt. Bzzzt.

"Your phone," Karam says. "Aren't you going to answer it?"

"It's my mom," I say in a dismissive tone.

"Maybe you should," he says, so I do.

"Hi, Mom. I'm busy. What's up...? What? No way! You're serious?" I jump up and perform a jig, phone pressed to my ear. "Dad's coming home! End of this week!" I holler to Karam and the whole world. "Okay, Mom. Yup, I'll be home in an hour or two, after parkour. Wow! Can't believe it! Thanks for calling me! Love you!"

Karam leaps up and boogies with me. We jive, hip hop, and rumba all at the same time, until finally I fall into his arms like some dance-star on a movie set.

Then we realize it's past time to show up at parkour.

CHAPTER ELEVEN

TOMMY GREETS US AT THE GYM DOOR. "KAZAM! BRONTE! Legendre has run out on an errand and ill-advisedly left Lillian the lily-livered sub in charge. And she, of course, has been persuaded to allow Valiant Vansh to teach us his polecat."

I laugh, still high from walking over here hand-in-hand with Karam, and the news of Dad's homecoming.

"The substitute could get fired if Legendre catches us," Karam half jokes, opening his laptop to check email.

"And we'll need the first-aid kit close by," I add, smiling as I tuck my backpack into a shelf cubicle near the door.

"Well, you're the only one in the club who's first-aid certified," Tommy says.

"True." I laugh. "Hey Karam, what's with doing work during parkour? Just toss your laptop in the cubby."

He raises his head and looks sharply at me, then starts typing like crazy. "Just need a minute. And I never trust those cubbies."

I sidle closer and pretend to read over his shoulder.

"Mind your own business!" he snaps, slamming the lid shut almost on his fingers. Then, "Sorry, sorry, sorry, Bronte. I just need a minute, okay?"

"Whatever," I say, shocked and hurt.

"Hey, everyone," Tommy shouts to the others, "let's all try Vansh's move!"

We move over to the room's three poles, Karam finally joining us.

"Vansh just wants to see us pole-dance, girls," Natalie jokes.

"Wouldn't mind," Dan kids back, prompting Jazz and Nat to leap up to the poles, wind themselves around them, and do some weird sexy moves. They collapse laughing on the mats.

"Never on Allah's green earth would I witness that in Aden," Karam says.

"Well, now you've got that out of your system," Vansh jokes.

"This thing you're practising is safe, right?" Lily the sub pipes up.

"Absolutely," Vansh assures her, winking at me.

Lily nods and wanders over to the water cooler to pour herself a cup of water and grab a folding chair and fashion magazine.

"So, I've set up overturned wooden boxes beside three poles," Vansh announces, rubbing his hands together excitedly.

I note two low boxes, one three feet away from its pole, the other five feet away. A third, four-foot-high box sits a scary five feet away from its pole.

"When you jump from box to pole," Vansh continues, "you need to get your feet against the pole first, just like a regular cat leap. Then your hands grab the pole. Let's start with your foot targeting: Stand next to the pole and extend a leg to touch the pole with the ball of one foot. You're going to practise just one foot at a time for now.

He watches us for a minute. "Good one, Bronte. Just a gentle kick against the pole. Okay, everyone, go ahead and try small jumps to your pole from the ground first, landing with both feet on it, one above the other."

Six people line up, two to a pole, taking turns running at it. They josh around as they try, slip, try again. Way harder than it looks, but I'm determined.

"Let me give you another demonstration," Vansh calls out, to our relief.

He steps up to the high box with the confidence of a performing acrobat. As he leaps effortlessly to the pole and sticks there like there are Velcro pads on his shoes and the pole, I notice he turns his feet so that his toes point to the same side as he lands. Yes, got it! Probably increases the odds of getting his feet against the pole, since it widens his contact surface for landing.

One by one, starting on the floor, we throw ourselves against the poles, sometimes bashing our poor bodies against them, mostly sliding right off like the metal is greased. But gradually, a few of us start getting it—sticking one out of five times, one out of four times... As we grow more confident or daring, we move to the boxes and try our luck from there, only to suffer more punishment from hitting the iron shafts.

Karam aces the low boxes a couple of times, but loses his cell phone from his sweatpants pocket in the process. His laptop, I notice, sits safely within view on a nearby chair.

"I'm going for the high box. Hold my phone for me a minute?" he asks.

"Sure."

"Interrupt me if it vibrates."

"Expecting a call from the queen?"

"Absolutely."

It takes four bruising tries, but my pride soars when Karam nails it on the fifth. Everyone breaks into clapping. He's the first to get the high one. He retrieves the phone from me and shoves it back into his pocket as he helps coach the others.

Soon, everyone's acing half their efforts on the low boxes. Then there's Dan, still working from the floor, struggling: As he goes at the pole from the mats, one or both feet are always slipping off it. At least he's still on ground level, so his feet keep hitting the mats, and he hasn't smashed into the pole yet. I pause to watch him.

"Dan," Karam speaks up, "you're jumping at the post with both feet pointed out to either side, like a duck. Try turning both of your feet to the same side."

"Quack, quack," Tommy teases Dan, who glowers back.

"Hey, I'm just ribbing you," Tommy assures him. "I think I've been doing the same thing."

Dan tries again, no closer to turning his feet the correct way. Head lowered, he punches the pole with his knuckles. Moody or what?

"Keep trying. Stay positive," Karam says, and turns to watch me. By now, I'm up on one of the two-foot-high boxes, doing successful plants almost every time. My feet tingle with excitement.

"That's my lady: a born traceuse," Karam says low enough that only I hear.

Ten minutes later, I notice Dan has stopped and is eyeing me. I'm well aware he has a crush on me. But he should stick to Jazel. The asshat is not even remotely my type, and I'm now taken. Totally taken.

As some of us have a break over at the water cooler, Dan marches to the high box and steps up onto it like an Olympic high diver waiting for cameras to turn his way.

"Um, Dan," Vansh says, "I suggest you try the lower boxes first."

"Nope, I've got this," he says, chin out and eyes narrowed.

When his body makes like it's about to leap, Karam rushes over to spot him. Sure enough, both of Dan's feet slip to either side as he lands five feet up the post. Instinctively, Karam pushes Dan's hips from the side, sending the Texan into a spin around the post, saving him from a terrible body-pole collision that would have fried his nuts.

Vansh and I are right behind Karam, but stand aside when we see he's got Dan.

Dan roars in anger as his feet reach the mat, then springs up to punch Karam. Karam seems to anticipate that, too, and moves aside in time to avoid it, sending Dan crashing into the box and rolling on the mat.

"You ruined it, asshole!" Dan says, face red, puffed, and now cut from the edge of the box.

"Boys! Stop this at once!" Lily commands, eyes big. "Dan, do you need a bandage?"

"Everything okay in here?" We swivel to see Omar Noori, of all people, standing beside the cubbyholes near the door. "I was just dropping in to see Julian."

"He's on an errand, and I'm in charge. Can I help you?" Lily asks.

"Nope, carry on," Noori says, exiting hurriedly.

"I'm out of here," Dan says, stalking over to the cubbies,

grabbing his bag, and leaving.

I watch Jazel's face fall, embarrassed for her man.

"Well done with the spotting, Karam," Vansh says, placing a hand on Karam's shoulder. "Maybe he'll thank you later."

"Don't count on it," I say, exchanging a look with Karam.

"Thanks, Vansh, but I'm bagged," Jazel says a few minutes later.

"Me too." Natalie gives an exaggerated sigh.

"Bagged from what?" booms Legendre's voice as he enters the room, looking haggard and distracted.

"Cat leaps," I say quickly.

"Cat leaps? Easy. Thought you could all do those already," he says with a touch of suspicion, looking from Vansh to Lily.

"They've been working hard, not that I know a cat leap from a tiger jump," Lily tries to joke, standing in front of the first-aid kit she grabbed after the attempted punch-out.

"I'm out of here too," I announce, moving towards the door. Then a flash of panic strikes me. "Hey, who took my backpack? It has my laptop in it! Oh, here it is," I say with relief, pulling it from its cubby. But not the same cubby, right? Huh. Whatever. "Karam, you ready to call it a day?"

"More than ready," he responds. We wave our goodbyes and walk out the door. "I don't need to be anywhere for an hour," he says. "Do you need to rush home to talk to your mom about your dad?"

"I should. She's expecting me and I'm pretty excited to hear about it, but I could text her that I'll be home a little later if you want."

"Great. Actually, I've been wanting to show you a special place." His face takes on a little color.

"A special place?" I tilt my head flirtatiously and give him a questioning smile.

"You've been saying that the Richland Mosque is your 'healing place.' I want to show you mine." His voice is low, like it's some important secret. It *is* a big deal, his wanting to share something like that with me.

"You're on. Is it warm?" I ask, pulling my red knitted hat down over my ears and shoving my gloved hands into my parka pockets.

"No, but it's not that cold today."

"Ha! You really have become an American, not complaining about the temperature."

"You're declaring me an American?" he enthuses, face lighting up even though he knows I'm kidding.

He reaches for my hand and we start up the steep, winding trail. Usually I jog it, but why rush the time Karam and I are together? The air smells fresh as we gain altitude. The wind picks up frosted tumbleweeds and rolls them ahead of us like wished-upon giant dandelion fluff.

We bound and stride among the roots and rocks of the rising trail, and I feel the sun behind the clouds just waiting to burst out and dance on the river below.

As we travel with the wind, I feel we've known each other for years, not weeks. This route, this scenery, Karam, and now the news of my dad: I've got a dizzying high. It makes me forgive the world for everything that was bringing me down before.

"Here," he says, as we reach the twin buttes divided by a four-storey-deep ravine. Rising from the floor of the gulch is the pathetic-looking red maple whose top, just a stone's throw from where we pause, stands solid and proud even in the breeze. On the other side, a lady is collecting plants just off the path that peters out before the east side's drop-off. She soon wanders out of sight.

Karam plops down on the wooden bench inscribed with hearts and initials, and tugs me gently down beside him. The panorama rolls out at our feet like a painting. To the north, huge, orange-roofed houses with squeaky-clean concrete driveways are perched on the long slope down to the broad, meandering river dotted by handsome bridges. Stretching even farther north, on the far side of the river, the downtown gives way to parks, warehouses, and faraway fields in brown, green, and yellow. Behind us, to the south, sit modest suburbs containing my house, Pearl's and Karam's place, the school, community centre, and library. We gaze for a while at the prettier, northern view.

"Stunning for a desert, isn't it?" he says. "I can almost imagine being back in Aden here, the river below being our bay."

"It is scenic," I agree, zipping my coat up to my neck. I glance sideways at the ravine. "Someone should build a little suspension bridge from this butte to the other one for a joined-up hiking trail."

"But then it would attract more walkers, and I wouldn't be able to come up and be alone."

"Guess what? You're not alone. I'm here too. So, why is this your healing place?" I put my arms around him and draw his face to mine.

Karam turns his face back to the water and swallows. "When I first came to Richland, every time I looked at the river, I used to see my family drowning."

My breath catches. "Tell me about it, Karam. You haven't said much about your family, or getting out of Yemen."

His hands grip his stomach. "I've never told anyone,

aside from my cousins. And they got the shortest description possible."

"Imam Taha says it's helpful to talk about things—otherwise, stress and difficult memories can get evil and toxic inside you."

"Toxic. That's the name for the fighting that drove my family from our home. Evil. That describes the men who threw my family and the other passengers overboard. Toxic and evil: nowhere near strong enough words to describe what Hussein—"

"Karam?" I whisper, my fingers catching his tears. "Hussein? Who's Hussein?"

He purses his lips and his face has gone gray, as if he has been caught talking in his sleep and can't remember what he said. I reach out to squeeze his hand and eventually he continues.

"My family was lucky. It's the people we left behind that need help," he says, his voice breaking. "My family wasn't lucky to drown, but we were lucky to get out of Yemen while we could. It took all my father's savings. In Aden, we climbed on a dhow—a cattle boat—for a sixteen-hour crossing to Djibouti across the Bab al-Mandeb Strait."

"The 'Gate of Tears,'" I translate softly.

"From there we made our way to Alexandria, Egypt, the starting point of what my parents called our 'cruise' to Italy. Even Jaleela, my favorite sister, believed it was going to be a vacation cruise."

He hesitates and wipes away a tear. "She was fourteen."

"I wonder if we were in Alexandria at the same time," I ponder, recalling Sarfraz and me watching illegal immigrants gathering on the beach at dusk through his binoculars. "Then what?"

CHAPTER TWELVE

WITH NO FURTHER URGING, KARAM EMBARKS ON A bone-chilling story.

At nightfall in Alexandria, we lounge in our seedy hotel room, the younger ones asleep, Father staring at his cell phone, sweat beads on his brow. Mother sits in her abaaya robe and hijab with the baby in her arms. She's as tense as a steel rod. Dad says to me, "You and I need to talk, alone."

"Okay." We walk out to the hotel balcony and sit on dusty chairs.

Dad sets down his briefcase and pulls a roll of wide grey tape from an inside jacket pocket, along with some sealable plastic bags.

"This is plumber's tape," he says.

I gaze at him. "Huh?"

"It's waterproof. Remove your shirt."

I yank off my T-shirt, mystified.

"You know I used to travel on business internationally about fifteen years ago, before it got difficult to leave Yemen?"

"Yes. You and Mother were in New York City, expecting me, when I arrived early."

The hint of a smile crosses his face. "Exactly. It is why you are the only one in our family with two passports. Yemeni and American."

"I know."

He opens his briefcase and fumbles through it before lifting out a set of documents and handing them to me.

My hand shakes only slightly as I accept the birth certificate and passports, a visa, a thick wad of American money in a rubber band, and a piece of paper with the address and phone number of Uncle Lando and Aunt Reem in the USA.

"Place all these in the plastic bag, seal it, put it inside another, and then tape them to your chest. Very, very securely."

I look up, startled, and suddenly get it. He thinks I'm the ticket to America? But what if they accept me and not the rest of them? How long before they'll allow us to reunite? And am I the only one he's trusting to carry my own documents?

Father hesitates, then places his hand on my shoulder. "You know it's a smuggling ship, not a cruise."

"Of course, Father. But I won't tell Jaleela and the others."

He tells me the name of the ship and its scheduled departure time tonight. I want to cover my ears, because I won't need that information if I'm with him.

The tape makes a loud tearing noise as I unroll some, press the bags to my chest, and create a giant square of grey anchoring it such that neither man nor fish could rip it off.

"Do not produce the birth certificate or American passport until we reach Italy. And if we become separated—"

I fasten my eyes on my father's tired-looking face.

"—get yourself to the American Embassy wherever you land, and they will help you reach my cousin. The rest of us will join you when we can."

"No, Father, I will stick like a leech to you all the way. We're family. We stay together." I use my firmest voice, trying to banish any hint of fear.

He nods, but his eyes won't meet mine. "I said only in the event we're separated." Leaning forward, he takes my head in his hands and pulls me to his chest. "Face forward, and live a full and honest life, son. You're a man, now. And never, ever support the beasts who try to recruit young people to fight supposed enemies of Islam."

"Of course not."

Recruiters for soldiers: It was one of the reasons we left. I wanted no part of the killing, but at sixteen, it was getting harder and harder not to get pulled in by the often fanatical agents. And gunmen were randomly killing anyone not siding with their particular group. If I'd ever had to decide, it wouldn't have been for any of the terrorist organizations, which commit unspeakable crimes that Allah will punish them for mercilessly in the afterlife, if not in this life.

Anyway, we go back inside. Thirteen of us are packed into the hotel room: my ten younger siblings, parents, and me. The youngest children are sleeping. Jaleela plays peek-a-boo with the rest to keep them calm. Whenever I started feeling nervous, I'd touch Jaleela's dimples. I don't know why, but it always calmed me, and her too.

"When do we leave on our cruise to Italy?" Jaleela asks.

For fun, I conjure up an image of a Disney-style cruise in first-class cabins where we run around and enjoy kids' play areas, shuffleboard, a swimming pool, cinemas, and a gym for practising parkour.

"Soon," Father replies with forced cheerfulness.

"A cruise will be fun," Mother says in a brave voice that reassures everyone but me. "We've never all been on one together."

When the phone rings, Father clamps it to his ear. "Yes? It's a go? Okay. Meet you there."

Gently, he organizes those old enough to carry the younger ones, and then kisses the top of Mother's head. I look away in embarrassment.

"It's time, everyone," he says. "And we're playing a game to see how quiet we can be on the way to the boat. Karam, follow right behind me."

I do as he says, carrying one of my brothers in my arms as my pack rides heavily on my back. We walk through dark laneways that make my pulse quicken, Dad on the cell the entire time.

As we near the harbour, I feel like half my body is about to stay behind in the Middle East. I don't know when, if ever, we'll be coming back. Freedom from the horrors of war may be what we've all wanted for months, but this opportunity to finally escape makes me feel like a sell-out and a cheat. Yemen, the Middle East, is what I've known all my life. It's where I've always belonged. If only I could take my friends with me, I keep thinking. But there's little time to reflect.

"Turn right here. Now straight," Father says, repeating directions from whoever he's talking with.

Breathing in the salty air to calm myself, I catch sight of a mini flotilla of small fishing boats with dim lights approaching the beach. Far offshore behind them, a dazzling array of lights identifies a convoy of ships. I'm guessing they're twelve miles out, in international waters. Which one is ours? Please let us reach it safely. Soon we will live somewhere safe and start a new life where there is no war. No bombs killing innocent people. No recruiters trying to turn children into soldiers.

Stars twinkle above, but my shoulders tighten in the stiff breeze blowing off the ocean. When a chubby man with a flat blue cap appears out of nowhere, Mother and I jump, but Father veers directly to him. They talk in low tones, the man gesturing to a group of about sixty people standing near the water, people like us, hands gripping small backpacks and children. A few are putting on cheap lifejackets.

"—five minutes," the man says, as he takes something Father hands him—money?—and melts into the night.

"Maybe we should have brought lifejackets," Father mumbles while herding us nearer to the water.

As we press into the rear of the throng staring out to sea, some people throw us wary looks. Several have phones pressed to their ears.

Lifejackets: I wonder who would need those on a short boat shuttle to a cruise ship. I realize I'm the only one in the family with a crinkly, uncomfortable square taped to my chest. Because I'm the oldest. Because I was born in New York City. Because we might get separated. I grip Jaleela's hand.

"There!" someone shouts, pointing to the group of fishing ketches moving towards us in the choppy waves.

Instead of waiting for the boats to reach shore or give us a signal, the excitable group reacts as if to a starting gun. My heart beats double time as people surge forward, wading from ankle- to hip-deep water. I could easily sprint past them all, but I stand steadfast with arms wrapped around my brother, wedged between my shaking mother and brave Jaleela, who is cradling the baby.

When the water reaches our calves, Mother pulls up the hem of her robe and freezes, unwilling to lift her feet from the sticky mud and tread farther.

"Karam!" Father shouts. "Give your brother to me, run like crazy, and save us space on one of the boats!"

I need no further urging. The people are in full panic, some tripping on the uneven bottom and being trampled by people behind. It's now every man for himself. Any families attempting to link arms find themselves torn apart by bodies lunging forward.

I may have a late start, but I'm fit and determined. With eyes locked on the nearest fishing boat, I crash through the water like a champion hurdler, then swim like a madman. When I reach it, I grip the upper edge—the gunwales—but so, too, do a dozen others.

As the vessel threatens to capsize, crewmen hit our wrists and fingers with oars and boat hooks. I cry out in pain, but swiftly swim to the far side and vault into the rocking boat. A mountain of wet, writhing bodies piles on top of me.

"Women and children first!" shouts someone to whom no one pays attention.

"Wait till we reach shore!" snarls a crew member, manhandling some of the smaller figures overboard. "No boarding till we say!"

I shrink into the centre, fists ready to fight anyone inclined to evict me, and I wait for the boat to draw closer to my family. But in seconds, despite the crew's efforts, the boat is filled with passengers way beyond any safe limit. So its operators turn it and head out to sea.

I scramble up and lean over the stern, shouting, "Father! Mother! Jaleela!"

"Here!" a distant voice responds, and I'm shocked but relieved to see them on a smaller yellow boat just behind mine, also overfull and heading seaward.

As we move farther from shore, the waves get choppier. Within minutes, some of my fellow occupants are heaving their supper over the sides. When my family's boat pulls near, I plant myself like a figurehead on the bow, eyes locked on them. Jaleela waves. I can't see her dimples in the near-dark.

Ten minutes later, our motor sputters and fails, and those around me groan. In the gloom, I watch my family's boat disappear ahead.

Er-er-er.

Please, Allah, let the outboard motor start.

Er-er-er-rrrum. Finally the starter kicks in, and we're off, now forming the tail end of the pack of dangerously over-loaded boats ploughing out to sea. Ahead, the ships' lights grow gradually brighter, silhouetting my family's boat. The waves toss us about, and whitecaps spit in our faces to remind us how low we're riding in the water. As the ships loom close, I remind myself to breathe slowly and evenly. Freedom is now within our grasp.

"What?" someone screams, as floodlights blind us from three boats lying in wait between the skiffs and the larger ocean-going vessels.

"Coast Guard!" shrieks a man who seems ready to dive off the boat to his death. "If they catch you, they shoot you on the spot or put you in prison and torture you."

My throat closes up, but all my concentration is focused on what's happening on the yellow boat well ahead. Distant blood-curdling screams and splashes reach our ears, as crew forcefully toss passengers off like they're undersized fish. They're throwing them overboard so the fishing boats aren't caught with any illegals aboard, I'm guessing. That way, they can claim to be innocent fishermen.

Horror, fear, and anger smother all reason. I stand up, intending to leap overboard, swim to the yellow boat, and rescue my struggling family members, but just then, our boat operator, who is far enough back to not yet be a Coast Guard target, guns the motor. The acceleration topples me into the bilge, where I thrash and scream. "No! I have to help my family!"

Someone holds me down as the boat careens at a crazy speed, parallel to the coastline and away from the Coast Guard vessels.

"No!" I pound my fists on the bottom, picturing Jaleela and my nine other siblings going under, my mother floating face first in the water, and my father, the only one who can swim, desperately trying to save them all. Why did he tell me to go ahead? I failed! I totally failed to save them spaces and haul them aboard. Their fate is my fault. I should be with them, pulling each to safety.

Maybe the Coast Guard will pick them up before they drown? Offer them blankets and hot tea? Let them board their ship or return to Yemen?

I know otherwise but cling to the image in desperation. My father spent his life savings getting us here. Surely it is not his destiny to drown within sight of a ship bound for Europe.

"We can fight the crew, hijack this boat," I say to the man nearest me, not loud enough that the crew can hear over the roaring outboard. "We outnumber them. We have to go back and help the people in the water."

"The men in charge of this boat are armed, idiot," he replies. "And who wants to go back to get arrested or shot? We're being taken to an island to wait it out. We'll get on that ship yet."

"How do you know?" I ask, stunned. "Do you work for them?"

"No, it's my fourth try getting out of Egypt," he says soberly. "I know the whole routine."

"Does the Coast Guard pick up people in the water?"

He looks at me as if measuring my ability to handle the answer. "Hardly ever in time," he finally says, and then turns away.

Shivers rack my body. Although the air temperature is mild, the wind creeps through our soaked clothing. I bury my head in my hands and try to block out a replay of the splashes and screams I heard from the yellow boat. Snot and tears drip on my already soaked jacket.

Twenty minutes later, the outboard slows, then stops a few feet from the slick, wet rocks of an island we can barely make out in the light of the half-moon.

"We'll come back for you as soon as we can," the crew say, helping us out onto the beach. "Keep your phones and flashlights off."

We file up to the highest point and sit like a ragged platoon of defeated soldiers. The blotted moon offers almost enough light to see each other. I squeeze in beside the man who spoke to me earlier.

"Will they come back?" I ask hoarsely.

He shrugs. "Sometimes yes. Sometimes no. Often not

before the Coast Guard or kidnappers or recruiters come get us."

"Kidnappers? Recruiters?"

"Kidnappers nab you and charge your smugglers money to give you back. Recruiters are religious extremists looking for strong young men to send on suicide missions and the like. Hide yourself well if they land, son."

Dad kept everyone afloat, I tell myself. They dodged the Coast Guard and drifted to the ship. Staff helped them aboard, and they are waiting there for me. The boat that dumped us here will return in time for my group to make the sailing. Everything's okay.

CHAPTER THIRTEEN

KARAM STOPS, LIKE HE HAS SCRAPED THE LAST OF HIS vocal cords dry. He has earned a pause, for sure, even if I'm dying for him to continue.

Tears form in my eyes. We cling to each other for a minute.

"Bastards!" I say of the fishermen who tossed passengers into the water. "But I thought the Coast Guard didn't care about refugees leaving Egypt, only those coming in."

"Usually they don't, and usually they're paid to look the other way anyway, but once in a while the politicians order them to do a roundup to make an example of people."

"What if some of your family got rescued? Maybe some are still alive?"

"Don't you think I've tried and tried to reach them? I've sent a hundred emails to Jaleela alone. Something inside me dies a little every time there's no answer, so I've stopped. None of my family could swim but Dad, and we didn't have lifejackets. Nobody in my family is in this world anymore, Bronte." The last words come out as a croak.

"And your boat was far enough back that you didn't get caught?"

"Yes, because of our motor problem. We got taken to that island to wait things out."

"Nelson's Island. I've heard of it, and seen it from rooftops in Alexandria. But it gets swept regularly by Coast Guard, doesn't it?" I lower my voice. "I've heard they don't care if they bring people back alive from there. Bringing back bodies means all the fewer to throw into prisons... So, what happened next?"

He goes quiet and looks away from me, then says in a bland voice, "We got rescued by a kind Coast Guard patrol. A Captain Hussein."

The name rolls off his tongue with bitterness.

I look at him sharply. Where have I heard him mention Hussein before? And why do I know this last bit doesn't add up?

Something Sarfraz said while using his binoculars that long-ago evening in Alexandria returns to me: "Oh, and some of the Coast Guard guys are double agents, as in they help so-called extremist recruiters find fighters from among the would-be escapees." Escapees like Karam.

"A *kind* Egyptian Coast Guard patrol? As in, they found you on the island, loaded you all on board, and illegally took you across the international line to ships they knew were run by people smugglers? Not likely. Not for free. Karam, what really happened?"

My changed tone turns Karam's face into a sea of pain. "Can I finish the story another time, Bronte? I really don't want to talk about this anymore."

"Of course, of course," I say in a more loving tone, placing my hands on his arm and trying to hide my disappointment. "I'm sorry. I'm also very, very glad you got rescued, so you could end up in Richland and we could meet—"

We're interrupted by his phone.

"Don't answer it," I say, maybe too aggressively.

He pulls the phone out of his pocket. "Why not?"

"It's probably them again: the sisters."

Panic registers on his face. "What do you mean 'again?'"

"They called when I was holding your phone, while you were doing Vansh's polecat."

"They called—and you didn't hand it to me? I told you that if it vibrated—"

"But these girls are nothing to you, right?" My voice is dark and challenging. My suspicious nature is all jacked up.

He stares at the text, then drops the phone to his lap like it has scorched him.

"Sorry, Bronte, but this is an emergency. Trust me. I'll explain later."

He grabs the phone, rises, and charges down the butte like a crazed bull. Towards the river, towards downtown. In one swift movement I'm up and racing after him, but he's clearly putting all his fitness training into losing me. He looks back once, his face stricken.

I'm winded and my legs are cramped up. He's faster and stronger than me, but if he thinks I'll call off the chase, he's wrong. I'm a girl who likes a challenge. Although the gap between us keeps widening, he's still in my sights as he arrives across from the downtown police station, where there's a strange circus of activity: patrol cars parked errati-cally, media threatening to spill over a rope erected by cops, and the arrival of a prisoner transport vehicle.

As I pull closer, panting heavily, I see Sheriff

MacDonald step down from the van, and officers open the rear doors. Two wildly frightened-looking girls are escorted out in handcuffs.

What? The fast-food girls?

"Karam!" the older one, Chloe, screams from across a sea of heads. Mascara streaks her tear-stained face, and her hair is sticking out at all angles, like she has been tugging on it.

"Karam!" yells Caitlin, as he seems to back up, set on losing himself into the crowd.

The sheriff gives Karam a fierce look—or did I imagine that?—then ushers his prisoners out of reach of the cameras and into the police station.

My teeth come down hard on my tongue. What's really between him and them? They're totally not his type, especially if they've done something to get themselves arrested.

Just as Karam is elbowing towards the rear of the crowd, and I draw within hearing distance, a camera sticks itself in his face, and a reporter shoves a mic up to his mouth, demanding, "Is your name Karam? Why are the girls calling for you? What's your connection with their alleged radicalization?"

Alleged radicalization? As Karam dodges to escape, my gut contracts, and I sink to the ground, too stunned to move.

Trust me. I'll explain later.

No secrets between us.

I want to chase after my fleeing boyfriend, but I've already spent every ounce of adrenalin I've got.

Sorry, Bronte, but this is an emergency.

Clearly, he tried to outrun me from the butte, to ditch me.

Does Imam Taha know Karam might— No! Karam's not tangled up in radicalization and recruiting. He left Yemen to escape that. There's some perfectly good explanation. What does Pearl know or suspect? Should I alert Imam Taha? No! I love Karam. I don't know when or how it happened, but I do. I want him to tell me the truth, and I want to protect him. But then, if he's involved in that stuff—. My head hurts so much I fear it's going to implode.

Karam whirls around and plunges down an alleyway, chased now by half a dozen media-types. When he reaches a high chain-link security gate at the end of the lane, I'm not surprised—maybe even vaguely proud as well as alarmed—when he jumps and pulls his hips to the top of it, leans his chest over the other side, and swings his legs over, leaving his confused pursuers to get their sound bites somewhere else.

CHAPTER FOURTEEN

Forgetting my promise to meet my mother, I walk to Pearl's house and sneak a peek in both the front window and Karam's room. He's not home. I need to talk to Pearl.

She answers my knock, looking startled. "Hey, Bronte. What's up? You look seriously winded. Out for a run?"

"Been at parkour club," I say briskly, nodding at her parents who start to rise from their seats in front of the TV. "Can I come in just for a few minutes? I've been trying real hard to work out a problem for computer science class, and I'm hoping you can help me."

"Sure," she replies cheerfully. "Let's go to my room."

She grabs us some cans of 7Up and a plate of home-baked coconut cookies from the kitchen before we head down the hallway.

"Wow, you're the best, Pearl. And you're way better at computer science than me."

"Yeah, well, calories always help with homework. How are you?" She motions to the chair at her small desk, beside which she has set the drinks and cookies, then plops herself down on her narrow bed and waits.

Do small talk first, I tell myself, head still spinning. "Pearl, I've hardly told anyone yet, but guess what?" I say in as bubbly a voice as I can manage.

"What?" she asks, face lighting up for me already.

"My dad's coming home! End of this week!"

She hugs me. "I'm so happy for you, Bronte. That's wonderful. Now you don't need to worry so much."

True. Not about Dad, anyway.

Somehow, I manage to remember a piece of our computer science homework, and Pearl being the patient teacher she is, she walks me through it in no time.

"Legendre sure makes us work hard," I comment, still wussying out of kick-starting the tough conversation.

"He does. Comes with his military background, I figure," she says.

"Yeah?" I'm stealing nervous glances at her unclosed door, wondering when to pull it shut for *the conversation*. "He was in Afghanistan, right?"

"Yes, with the French forces under NATO, he told me. He was Special Forces, and most of his comrades got killed."

"Ouch," I say, genuinely sorry for Mr. Legendre. "So he risked his life trying to get rid of terrorists there?"

"Yes, and then after he returned, he found that lots of French citizens are prejudiced against Muslims in the military."

"Wait. Legendre is Muslim?"

"You didn't know?"

"Um, I've never seen him at the mosque, and he has never said anything. And you haven't mentioned it before."

"He goes to the mosque sometimes. And I see him enter

the boys' prayer room at school, obviously. You will too, when you start your šalāt, your daily ritual prayers, Bronte."

Her tone is halfway between encouraging and scolding. But I have way too much on my mind to get into that right now.

"Uh-huh," I manage, with a glance at the clock.

"Anyway," she continues, "I did a paper on it. Did you know there are several thousand Muslims in the American military—and some have given their lives—but almost half of all Americans question their loyalty, especially in the Gulf, Iraq, and Afghanistan Wars? It was probably not that different for Mr. Legendre in France, when he finished his service."

"That's really interesting, Pearl, but I'm here to talk to you about something else." She raises an eyebrow as I leap up to close the door quietly.

"I thought so," she says pointedly. "Is it about your masjid classes? How are they going?"

"Fine," I say, eyes on her wall decor.

"You need to be sincere about learning Islam, not playing some game," she says, eyes narrowed.

My breath hitches and I squeeze my eyes shut. "Pearl, I'm here about Karam. Something's going on with him that's not okay."

"Like what?" she asks, her voice a little cool.

"Text messages that seem to spook him. Hanging out with other girls on the sly but claiming he's only showing them websites on Islam. Talking on the phone in frightened tones to someone. Not letting anyone get near his laptop, and—"

"Bronte, maybe you're imagining things." The tone is two degrees warmer than icy. "I know you're stressed out about home and all, but Karam's fine or I'd know. Anyway, I'm not interested in getting between you two. I don't want to hear this. I'm his cousin first, your acquaintance second."

Acquaintance, she said. Not friend. Because she doesn't trust my reasons for going to the masjid. I don't blame her. I don't even know what I'm doing there sometimes. Staying away from my mother and former school friends? Trying to understand Karam and Pearl better? In need of a new community? Or trying to manage my stress? But that isn't where this conversation needs to go.

"Pearl, you have to hear me out. Those are the little things. An hour ago, Karam got a phone call while I was with him, and his face turned white and he ran away in a panic."

"I said I don't want—"

I drop my voice in case her parents are on the other side of the door. "He ran downtown. I followed him all the way to outside the police station, where Sheriff MacDonald was unloading two prisoners – the girls Karam has been hanging out with. They were handcuffed and called out to him. Then a reporter tried to ask Karam if he was involved in their attempted radicalization."

Pearl's face goes from dubious to concerned. Her pretty mouth drops open and there's silence as we both glance at the closed door.

"W-what did he say, and where is he now?" she whispers.

"He ran away from the reporters and me. I don't know where he is."

Pearl takes out her phone and punches in a text message, then stares at the screen, eyes blinking rapidly. Like he's going to answer immediately.

I lean in. "Pearl, I know you don't really trust me, but we both care about Karam. We need to—"

"To what?" she demands, her face pale, hands falling to her sides.

"Look in his room?" comes out of my mouth.

"That would be dishonest, wrong." She's trembling.

"Yes, but maybe there's some reasonable explanation. Or maybe he's in trouble and we can help him."

To my surprise, she rises, opens the door a crack, and checks out the hallway. I stand behind her, my backpack dangling from one shoulder, ready to say I'm heading out if her parents ask. The hall's empty, the TV still blaring from the living room. Pearl clasps my hand and leads me to Karam's room. As she shuts the door gently behind us, I beeline for his desk while she bites her lips and stares uncertainly at his bookshelf.

His drawers are mostly empty. Pens, pencils, erasers, an Arab-English dictionary. But in the bottom drawer, so warped I have to wrestle to open it, there's a thick, printed document rolled up with a rubber band.

I tug out the pages and snap off the band. When I see the title, my jaw drops.

"Pearl!" I say, and she begins reading over my shoulder.

Recruiting Manual

- *Hold seminars on Islam to attract potential recruits.*
- *Seek out nonreligious people, because they are easier to manipulate.*
- *Young people who have difficult relationships with their parents are also ideal for recruiting.*
- *Look especially for "outsiders" who are*

vulnerable, isolated, and seeking meaning in their lives. The less they know about Islam, the better...

As I speed-read more, my blood pressure surges. Then footsteps sound in the hallway.

"Pearl? Bronte?" Aunt Reem calls out.

Pearl shoves the document inside her tunic and picks up a stapler from Karam's desk. As she turns to the door, I reach for his laptop and slide it into my backpack. I can figure out his password later and get to the bottom of this.

"Just borrowing Karam's stapler for some homework we're working on," Pearl informs her mother as we step out the door.

"Oh! Okay. I've made some tea if you want any."

"Thanks," I say, "but I'd better get going."

"I'll have some in a minute, Mother, thanks."

As Pearl's mom retreats to the kitchen, Pearl turns to me, face flushed. "I will take this to Imam Taha. You will say nothing to anyone, including Karam. Agreed?"

"Agreed," I say, the laptop feeling as heavy as an anchor in my backpack.

"Mom!" I burst through the front door. "So sorry I'm late. So excited about Dad! Tell me everything!"

She hugs me, smiles, smoothes back my hair. "No problem. Everything okay?"

"Everything's fine. Is that lasagne I smell? Oooo, you're the best."

"It's a little overdone, maybe, but I'll tell you everything while you eat."

After lasagne and a long, lively chat, I beg off to my room to do homework. Definitely not the kind of homework Mom would approve of. First, I try a bunch of passwords to get into

Karam's laptop. "Yemen," "Aden," "parkour," "traceur," even "Bronte."

I feel crazy being just one word away from seeing what Karam might be up to. But it was stupid and wrong, stealing his computer. *What possessed you, Bronte?*

To diffuse my frustration and guilt, I go back to my computer, straight to my social media, and click on the mysterious message guy. His internet name is "True Caliph," and there's a generic grey silhouette where his photo should be. Mystery dude. I read over all his messages, which remain unanswered. The first one came right after I posted that photo of myself in Pearl's hijab—for ten minutes.

Dear Bronte:
I like your photo. You look like a girl who is at peace with serving Allah. Are you new to Islam? I wish you a beautiful day.
True Caliph

Dear Bronte:
I would really like to hear from you. I should tell you that I live in Richland and have seen you out doing parkour. Good for you! Don't let anyone tell you this is not a sport for Muslim girls. It requires the kind of fitness and bravery that is only to be admired.
How long have you been a sister?
True Caliph

Dear Bronte:
I know you're shy about returning my messages, but I just want to say I admire you for your recent conversion and would like to encourage your search for answers. Maybe we

could just talk about Islam? And what do you think about
mujahideen and *hijrah*?
True Caliph

I know that *mujahideen* means people involved in jihad,
which can but doesn't always mean fighting, because jihad also
refers to an internal struggle to perform acts of obedience for
Allah. And *hijrah* refers, more or less, to Islam's golden age—
the eighth to thirteenth centuries—which some radicals think
is due to be reinstated. That last line makes me suspect he is a
recruiter, itching to radicalize me. Now that I've read Karam's
manual, I can see why. They like the newly converted, especially girls. And what army, however perverted their cause,
wouldn't want a strong, fit girl to carry around an AK-47?

If "True Caliph" knows I do parkour, maybe he also
knows other things about me: that I have a messed-up family,
am not religious, don't know much about Islam, am sort-of an
"outsider" lately at school—and that I could check off lots of
the other boxes on their "wanted" list for ideal recruits. So
sick.

A terrifying thought occurs to me, making me put my
hand to my mouth: Could True Caliph be Karam? I keep
reading the messages.

Dear Bronte:
I would like to get to know you better. Also, where Islam is
concerned, I would like to help you lead the life waiting
for you.
True Caliph

Dear Bronte:

Are you there? Please put me out of my pain by answering, even if it's to say you don't want to be my friend.
True Caliph

After some hesitation, I type, "Dear True Caliph, who are you, really?"

Spookily, he answers within thirty seconds, almost like he has been sitting there, fingers hovering over his keyboard, waiting for me all these weeks.

Bronte!
You've made me the happiest man ever by replying. I'm entirely free to message with you right now.
True Caliph

I shut down the computer, back away, and all but run downstairs to my mother.

"Mom, watch a movie with me? I'm not sleepy." I plop down on the sofa beside her, not wanting to move even an inch away from her warm, comforting body. It's like my room upstairs is now haunted.

"Sure, Bronte. That would be lovely. Not going out with Karam tonight? Lucky me! You will bring this new beau around for me to meet sometime, though, right? Maybe have him over for dinner next week, so your father can meet him too?"

"Mom."

"Yes, Bronte?"

"I'm breaking up with Karam. Maybe."

"Oh, Bronte!" She enfolds me in a big hug. I appreciate that we've mended our relationship, that she's my warm and loving mother again. I cling to her a long time but don't let myself cry.

"I'm so sorry. It seemed to me like you were over the moon. Okay, tell me all about it. Okay if I make us some popcorn?"

"Popcorn would be good." I tell her nothing, of course.

CHAPTER FIFTEEN

"Bronte, honey, you'd better get up. You need to read the newspaper before you go to school."

I sit up in bed abruptly, glance at my bedside alarm clock, then take in my mother's grave face. She's holding the morning's paper.

I stare at the headline: "Radicalized in Richland!"

There's a photo of Chloe and Caitlin being cuffed at the airport, another of them calling out to Karam as they arrive at the police station.

And the line underneath the headline: "Local girls allegedly radicalized for overseas terrorism are arrested at airport. Could there be a teen terrorist recruiter in our midst?"

My throat feels tight, like someone is strangling me. "Oh my god," I say, staring at my mother in disbelief.

"This is the Karam you were dating?" she asks in a shrill voice, her whole body shaking. "This is maybe why you're breaking up?" Her voice rises to a shriek. "Darling, you're scaring the hell out of me! What on earth—"

"Let me read it!" I command, grabbing the thing. She lowers herself to the edge of my bed like she might faint if she doesn't sit, and waits, speechless for once.

The article goes on to report that the girls had stolen their father's credit card to book a flight to Turkey, from which terrorist contacts were to smuggle them into Syria. This was explained in a note their parents found an hour after the delayed flight was to take off. The parents phoned police, who had already pulled the girls out of the airport security line and arrested them—within sight of a newspaper photographer who happened to be at the airport.

"Shit" is all I can say.

"Did you know this about Karam?" Mom asks, her voice uneven, her eyes accusing.

"Know what?!" I reply, teeth clenched.

She looks frightened of me for a second, like when things were bad between us. "Why don't you get up and get dressed? I'll fix us some breakfast," she says unevenly.

"Thanks," I manage to say, reading on. There's speculation about the girls' link to the "Muslim Arab boy" they cried out to while being escorted into the Richland police station for questioning—a "local boy and alleged recruiter who now appears to be in hiding."

I take a shower and throw on some clothes, then grab the paper and head downstairs, where Mom is waiting, eyeing me like a court judge, while buttering toast.

There are quotes from the local imam about his constant efforts to nip radicalization in the bud. He also verifies that the Yemini boy in question, Karam Saif, attends the local mosque.

"I have no reason to suspect Karam of any evil-doing, and it's important to remind people that in America, one is innocent until proven guilty," Imam Taha is quoted as saying.

My sweaty fingers curl the edges of the paper, as Mom hands me toast on a plate. I start reading aloud.

"Three Rivers High School Principal Mark Nelstrop confirmed that Karam Saif attends school there. 'He has never been any trouble,' Nelstrop said. But a classmate of Karam's, Dan Lyon, told *The Press*, 'Some of us have suspected him for a while, ever since he led an information session on Islam at the local community centre.'"

My head drops to the table. I want to sink through it, through the kitchen floor, and down through the entire radius of the Earth to wherever I'd come out the other side.

"Talk to me, Bronte," Mom says tensely. "And are you going to school today? You're running late already, you know."

Biting into the toast, sipping lukewarm coffee, I toss the paper aside. "I'm going upstairs to check my computer." She opens her mouth to object, then gets that unsure, scared-of-her-own-daughter look again and stares worriedly after me.

Shit and double shit. My Richland High friends' social media pages are as covered in messages as a urinal. And at the top, there's a photo Natalie has released of Karam talking with Chloe and Caitlin at her party.

"PROOF!!!" the line beneath it declares.

Below, someone has posted: "F—in' amazing, a crazy terrorist right here @ 3 Rvrs!"

There are many more comments, of course, and a record number of hits from my classmates viewing them:

"Kill all the Moslems! Bar them from our school!"

"Who else was he going to convert?"

"Is Bronte a terrorist too? How come she's not in school

today? BTW, she speaks Arabic. Maybe she got radicalized in Egypt last year."

"Free trip to Syria to decapitate people, folks! Just call Karam, the devil."

"Sooo scary. I even sat next to him in math class!"

"My parents won't hardly let me go to school now. Like, we're all going to be blown up or something?! How could this happen in Richland?"

"I knew those girls. Total losers. But nobody should get lured and sucked in like that. They'd've gotten themselves killed. Like, made into suicide bombers or something."

"Get real, you people. No one has convicted Karam. What if it's someone else, and that someone else is still in our school?"

"Then why's Karam hiding, idiot? 'Cause he knows we'll KILL HIM. Maybe even cut off his head and make a video of it."

"No wonder he did parkour. Gave him moves to fight anyone who tried to stop him, maybe. The police should be looking into who else in that club might be into Islam."

I want to vomit up the piece of toast, the messages are so vicious and idiotic. I wonder if the kids from the mosque are all staying home, frightened. I wonder if Imam Taha has security guards on high alert. I wonder if the parkour club members are taking some of the heat. Where the hell is Karam and why is he hiding? What's the real story? And did Pearl talk to Taha?

"Where r u?" I text Karam with trembling thumbs.

Most of all, I hurt for Pearl and her parents. They didn't do anything to deserve this. Do they wish they'd never taken Karam in? No, they're probably a hundred percent convinced of his innocence. I picture his Uncle Lando mobbed by reporters on his lawn, fist raised, shouting, "Leave us in peace!"

Me, I'm just utterly confused. Karam agreed to "no secrets." Was that a lie? Friends who lie, cry. Die? Say goodbye?

Just as things were getting so good, it's ruined now. Karam and me being an item had pretty much already hosed my friendship with Jazel and Natalie.

Even if Karam turns out to be innocent, this will never go away. Not from the mosque, not from Pearl's family or from Karam. People are too riled up, too eager to believe crap.

I check my phone messages.

Principal Nelstrop: "Bronte, please come to my office so we can talk."

Imam Taha: "Bronte, please come see me during this difficult time."

Mr. Noori: "Phone or visit the mosque, Bronte."

Mr. Legendre: "Bronte, are you okay? If there's anything I can do, let me know."

Pearl: "Coming to school 2day? U ok? Have news re Taha talk."

Okay, must get with Pearl ASAP.

I text Karam again: "Explain. No lies. Or we're done."

I bury my head in my hands and picture Karam hiding and alone. All alone in a country he thinks hates him. A country that insists on believing that the desperate refugees fleeing from terrorists are the terrorists themselves. Why is it "be killed or be hated" just because he had the misfortune of living in a country gone bad? I picture him miserable, wishing he'd drowned with his family. Or *is* he a recruiter? It's not looking good, Kazam.

I remember his father's last words to him: "Think positively even in the face of disaster. Face forward, and live a full and honest life, son. You're a man, now. And never, ever support the beasts who try to recruit young people to fight supposed enemies of Islam."

I picture his family thrashing about in the water, screaming for help, sinking. And how he told me that his first few months here, he relived that scene every time he looked at our river. He blames himself for their dying.

"Why should I have lived when they didn't?" he questioned after telling me his escape story. "Why me and not Jaleela, who was pure and good? My heart breaks every time I remind myself I will never see or talk to them again."

I imagine his younger sister, the one with dimples. And how he'd lift his hand to touch them, something that calmed both of them.

I turn to Karam's laptop again and try "Richland" and "Jaleela." Nope. Still haven't guessed his damn password. Gritting my teeth, I try "Chloe" and "Caitlin." Neither of those, I'm happy to see.

Okay, what are his favourite moves in parkour? I try them all: kong, cat-pass, side-flip, reverse-vault, precision, webster, and lachè.

Forget it. Total waste of time. I check my phone again. No reply. He doesn't care enough to answer me, or else he has been thrown into jail with his radicalized girlfriends, no phone access allowed. If he was allowed one call, would he even choose me? What would I even say?

"When can we talk?" comes Pearl's text.

Poor Pearl. She's at school, and probably paying big-time for her bravery in showing up.

I rise and squint out the window towards Three Rivers High School, not quite visible in the sleet. Yeah? Well, she has something to tell me. And she needs someone to stand up to all this with her. The more crap we get thrown at us, the faster this will die down. Girls who stick together don't get kicked together. Okay, my poetry skills are on the lam.

"OMW," I text Pearl. I throw on my clothes, gather up my schoolbag, and march downstairs.

"You're going to school," Mom observes with approval that fails to hide concern. "Bronte, did you know that Karam —? Did he ever try—? Will you talk to police—?"

"Yes I'm going to school, Mom. Hiding is for losers. Dad wouldn't want me to stay at home. I'll explain it all sometime, but not now. He might be innocent, you know."

She stares at me, makes a feeble attempt to hug me, finally smiles tightly. "That's my girl. Okay. I'm headed out to do some errands." She means running around getting things ready for Dad's return: buying his favourite foods, getting her hair done.

CHAPTER SIXTEEN

I step out the door into the icy weather and point my boots towards school. Let people sling what they want at me. Karam's not my BF anymore anyway. Just another mistake, like Sarfraz. I dab my eyes, take a deep breath, and propel myself forward.

The minute I enter the school corridor I see Dan and Pearl. Dan and Pearl? Not a good combo. I sprint towards them.

"Leave me alone!" I hear Pearl's firm voice as she tries to dodge him.

He lifts her tunic. "Just wanted to make sure you're not packing any explosives under there."

Pearl's wounded eyes spot me.

"How dare you!" I shout at Dan.

He whirls around, eyes wide, then sees a teacher approaching us and flees. A bell rings, giving Pearl and me just seconds to bolt to class.

"Imam Taha says Karam is safe but can't communicate

with anyone," she whispers, eyes watery. "That's all I know, Bronte."

"Thank you," I say, hugging her before we hustle to our respective classes. I feel confused and stricken. Surely Pearl learned more than that? But she wouldn't lie to me, that I know for sure.

"Bronte," says Mrs. Lau, the math teacher, as I slip into a dead-silent classroom of students staring at me. "I just gave out a pop quiz. Please be seated." She hands me mine.

A quiz: just what I need. Jazel is staring full-on at me from her desk, a trace of sympathy on her face. She's also trying to measure where I'm at.

"Karam and I are finished," I whisper to her and Natalie, as I slide in behind them.

Jazel's hand reaches back and squeezes mine. I'm sure she means it to be warm and reassuring, but to me, it feels lukewarm and oily. Like our friendship has conditions attached—dumping my Muslim boyfriend being one of them.

Imagine if she knew I'd been attending prayers and Muslim education sessions at the mosque, wearing a hijab? Or chumming with Pearl, who has way more going for her than the entire cheerleading squad piled on top of one another? Too bad Pearl's not here in my math class right now. Thank goodness Dan isn't.

Natalie nods to me, but I give her a cold stare. She certainly drew a lot of venom by posting that photo of Karam and the girls at her party. And she declared it was proof. Proof of what? That she's a wicked witch? Doesn't she realize that once out, poison doesn't always lose its toxicity? And sometimes it takes down the person who released it in the first place?

The math quiz, Bronte. Pay attention, girl. The door

opens a crack. Everyone lifts their heads. It's the principal, speaking in low tones to Mrs. Lau and jabbing a finger towards me.

Please don't call me out of class. Please leave me alone.

"Bronte," Mrs. Lau says, as everyone stares at me again. "Principal Nelstrop needs a word with you."

"It's nothing to do with me," I pronounce before he even closes his office door. I sit the other side of his desk with arms crossed in the "bad kids" chair. "And I have no idea where he is."

Principal Nelstrop sighs, seats himself, and looks at me sadly. "This has nothing to do with Karam."

I look at him, eyes narrowed.

"Your mother phoned. She has just heard from your father's employer. A network executive."

I press my fingernails into my palms and squeeze till it hurts.

"I think you need to go home and be with your mother."

"Is she okay? What's—?"

"It's— It's your father." Principal Nelstrop is looking at me uncomfortably.

"Tell me now. Don't make me wait till I get home and see my mother, please."

"He has been kidnapped." He says the words reluctantly.

My mouth goes so dry I can't even swallow. I'm staring at the principal. "No, he's coming home this week," I say defiantly.

He leans forward, reeking of sympathy. "Bronte, do you want me to call a taxi or find someone to walk you home?"

"I— I— No thanks," I say, rising and stumbling out the office door. I walk in a daze to my locker, hear the tap-tap of hail on a skylight overhead, look up at it, and feel myself falling back.

"Bronte? Bronte?" It's a deep male voice, and it sounds concerned. "She has come to. I'll take her to the office."

I feel arms raise me from a cold cement floor, and an elbow support me as I stagger forward. People seem to be crowded around me, but they're just forms, no one with an actual face.

"Make way," the deep voice says, and I lean into its owner. I'm led somewhere quiet, somewhere there's a little cot with a blanket. The cup of water he gives me tastes good.

"Bronte, it's Dan," he says.

My eyes fly open.

"You fainted, but you seem okay now. Mr. Nelstrop is calling your mom. I'm here if you need anything, 'cause I was the first to find you."

"Dan," I say foggily. Then a flash of anger makes me bolt up to a sitting position. Dizziness knocks me back down to the cot. "Dan! Why were you being mean to Pearl? And why did you talk to reporters about Karam?"

He sighs, his arm still on mine. I feel too weak to shake it off.

Ignoring the first question, he addresses the second. "I guess I just wanted to see if my name would get in the paper. Bronte, Jazz just told me you broke up with him."

The fog in my head is clearing. "Well, doesn't news travel fast around here?"

"Bronte, you know I really like you. I've never figured out why you don't like me."

"No? You tell me why you hate Muslims, and I'll tell you why I hate you."

His eyes go wide. He looks around as if worried someone might have heard me.

"I'm a Christian, and Muslims are trying to take over the free world, Bronte. You know that."

"A tiny percentage of them are deluded enough to think they are, yes, Dan. The rest of them want nothing to do with — What are we doing here, anyway? Aren't we supposed to be in class?"

I try sitting up again.

"Bronte." Principal Nelstrop and Mr. Legendre enter the room together and stand tall over me.

"Oh my god," I say, throwing Dan's hairy arm away from me and staring at the men. "My mom! My dad! I have to get home! That's where I was going!"

"Bronte, I won't let you walk home alone," Principal Nelstrop says. "Mr. Legendre is free this period. I've asked him to accompany you. Dan, you're excused to get to class. Okay?"

Dan looks crushed but stands up reluctantly. "You didn't answer my question, Bronte," he says bravely.

"I dare you to talk to the priest or minister who were at Karam's seminar," I say to him in what I hope is a calmer tone.

"About what?"

"Islamophobia."

I don't get a chance to see his expression, because Principal Nelstrop lays his hands on Dan's shoulders and steers him firmly out of the room.

"I'm sorry to hear about your father, but I'm sure the television network will get him out in no time," Mr. Legendre says, kind eyes on my face. "Take it easy. There's no hurry. Your mother knows I'm bringing you home."

I rise slowly. His strong arms give me confidence. He's one handsome, thoughtful dude. I bundle up and we walk out the school's front doors.

"It seemed like you were under a lot of stress even before this call about your dad—and before today's, um, news. Am I right, Bronte?"

I sigh heavily and lean on him. "You don't know the half of it."

"Tell me anything you'd like to share," he says kindly.

He's such a good listener that by the time we're halfway home, I'm telling him about Mom's abrupt decision to leave Egypt, my parents' sort-of breakup, Mom and me butting heads, Dad's dangerous work, and even Sarfraz and me. I steer clear of mentioning Karam, but talk about how Imam Taha has helped me, and how I've been attending the mosque.

"Pearl only just told me you're Muslim," I say carefully.

He looks surprised for a second, then smiles. "Yes I am, and I'm glad you've found someone to talk to, and some peace from your troubles, Bronte. Do you know if Karam is okay?"

I stare at the ground and slow down. Pearl's sliver of info is confidential. And I'm not about to tell him what Pearl and I found in Karam's drawer. "No idea. And I don't know what was up with him and those girls. I stole his laptop from his house to find out."

Legendre looks at me sharply, and I lower my head.

"I know it was a terrible thing to do, but I had to find out."

"And?" he asks gently, even though we both know it's none of his business.

"I don't know his password, so I can't get in. Need password-cracking software."

"You should return it to him, Bronte. That would be the right thing to do."

I nod, ashamed, then look up and halt. "You could help me, being a computer science guy, couldn't you, Mr. Legendre? You could figure out his password?"

He hesitates, frowning. "I could, but that would be illegal and immoral. And wrong for your relationship with Karam, who may be entirely innocent."

"You think?" I ask distractedly. Someone still thinks he's innocent, even after what has been in the papers? We walk in silence for several minutes, till we reach my house. "It's either you or Mr. Noori who could help me find Karam's password. Karam isn't around to give the laptop back to, anyway."

He shrugs and gives me a defeated look.

"Okay, I'm going upstairs to get it, Mr. Legendre. Wait here. It'll be just between you and me."

I open the door, hear Mom crying, rush upstairs, then come back down. My teacher is standing awkwardly on the front porch. I shove the laptop at him.

"I'll take it home with me and give you the password and the laptop back tomorrow, then," he offers.

"Thanks, Mr. Legendre."

"They'll rescue him, Mom," I say as hopefully as I can, trying not to let on how frightened I am.

"They haven't had a reporter kidnapped for three years," she says, her face a puffy mess, her new perm a stringy mop. "His team is always assigned military escort."

"But there are people on it, you said. Experts in this stuff. And he's really valuable to them."

"Damn Yemen. It was too dangerous a place to go. I

begged him not to take the assignment."

I say nothing, trying to forget their constant arguing in Egypt.

"He was going to be home this week."

"He was," I agree, and we hug one another.

After Mom has drifted off to sleep, I text Karam once again.

"Dad kidnapped. Use ur contacts 2 find him?"

Then I flip open my laptop with trembling fingers.

Dear True Caliph:
When would you like to chat?
Bronte

Just as I press send, an email comes in that makes me break into a sweat.

Dear Bronte:
How are you? I miss you so much. Please forgive me for the way I acted when we parted. I thought it might make things easier, but now I am deeply ashamed.
I finished my camp, and although I have found a job, I have too much free time to think about you, and I think about you day and night. I never realized how much you meant to me, and I believe we are still meant to be together. Please, please write me so I know you are alive and well, and maybe still have feelings for me?
All my love,
Sarfraz

It takes a split second to begin a reply to the love of my life.

CHAPTER SEVENTEEN

An hour later, I check my phone, social media, and email again. A message from Karam in my email makes me cry out.

I'm in hiding but safe. I'm not allowed to contact anyone, but I'm defying that right now. I want you to know that I'm not what the papers say, and that I miss you, and my aunt and uncle and Pearl. I also have to share some incredible news I received just an hour ago. My sister Jaleela is alive! I'm no longer so alone in the world.

The letter she wrote me, and my answer to her, are below. I just had to share them with someone, and you more than anyone will understand what this means to me. Please be happy for me and trust me for now.

As for your father, I'm so upset for you that he has been kidnapped. You were so happy he was coming home! But Yemen? It's open season year-round on foreign journalists there. A high-level kidnapping like that— What are the chances his TV network and the government will negotiate his release? What a mess. I wish I could help, but there's nothing I can do, not even come and hug you. I'm sorry, Bronte."

I stare at his message. In hiding? Why? Not allowed to tell me anything? Screw you. You're not what the papers say? But you're obviously reading them from your hiding spot. You miss Pearl and all—but you're not contacting them, and you're letting the media I heard is parked on their lawn drive them crazy. Jaleela alive? Nice for you, but... I hate you. I love you. I believe you. I'm scared of you. I'm finished with you. Come out and make it alright. Or soon it'll be me and Sarfraz.

Moist fingers steaming my screen, I scroll on to read Jaleela's letter.

Dear Karam:

Alhamdulillah! Praise Allah you are alive, and you have even reached America! I cried tears of joy when I first got access to all your emails this very morning.

It was today I was finally released from prison here in Alexandria and driven to a nearby refugee camp.

We weren't allowed communication of any kind while locked up. Yes, dearest brother, I am alive, though not so well. I got very ill in prison, which was an abominable place, and am in the camp's infirmary now. I am weak, but news of your escape gives me new strength.

Father saved me from drowning when we were thrown from the boat. He got me to the Coast Guard vessel, then went back to help Mother and the others. He never returned, and I was forced to identify all their bodies the next day. Karam, that was the worst moment of my life. I am so sorry to deliver you that news, though you must have feared the worst.

But brother, my dearest brother, you and I have survived, and

Allah must mean us to be together. Can you come to Alexandria and rescue me from this awful camp? Can you bring me to America, so we can live together?
I cannot write more. I am too tired, and there is a line-up of angry people waiting for the only public computer in the infirmary.
I send you hugs and thank you for all your efforts trying to reach me. In shaa Allah, we will soon be together.
Love,
Jaleela

Dearest Jaleela:
My happiness is beyond description to hear from you.
Though you have confirmed my deepest fears, this is offset by knowing you are still alive.
Jaleela, I will find a way to get to Alexandria as soon as possible, to release you and nurse you back to health. Please trust that I will be there as fast as I can.
Alhamdulillah, praise Allah you are alive, my very dearest sister,
Love,
Karam

And then Karam's closing message to me: "I am determined to bring Jaleela to Richland so we can start our new life together. But she's ill. I need to be at her side, holding her hand, giving her strength, and making sure she gets the care she needs. When I bring her to Richland, she and you and Pearl will become best of friends. Maybe she'll help Pearl break out and be more adventurous. She'll charm Aunt and Uncle big-time, and they'll have forgiven me by then.

Jaleela will like the river here, and will soon be strong

enough to walk all the way to the top of the twin buttes. We'll hold a *janaza* there to honour our lost family and pray for Allah's blessings on them in the afterlife.

Then I'll introduce her to Richland: fast-food (minus non-halal meat), bowling, and Western movies. All the teen boys at the masjid will have an instant crush on her, but I'll vet every single would-be suitor in town. Be happy for me, Bronte. Karam

CHAPTER EIGHTEEN

"Pearl, I'm so glad you were free this afternoon," I say the next day, out of breath from my run over to her house after school hours, having promised my distraught mother I'd be back shortly. "I so need a friend to talk to."

She gives me a warm hug. "I'm always here for you, sister. Have you heard from Karam?"

"No." I can't meet her eyes, not just because I'm lying this time, but knowing I stole Karam's laptop right from under her nose the last time I was here.

"Nor me," she says sadly.

"Hi, Bronte," Aunt Reem greets me, producing a plate of small cakes. "It's always good to see you. Any word on your father?"

"Not yet. Thank you, Mrs. Saif," I say, accepting the plate graciously and following Pearl to her room.

"How are you doing?" I ask Pearl, whose blouse looks like she has been sleeping in it, and whose hair looks uncombed.

"I am doing as well as can be expected," she replies,

lifting her chin in an effort to reassure me, but there are bags under her eyes. "I've been praying for Karam. This has been difficult for the masjid, yet everyone there is praying for him."

I sigh and study the floor.

"I believe with all my heart that my cousin is innocent."

No comment on that. I just look up and give her a little hug.

"So you've heard nothing on your father?"

"Well, yes and no. But what I tell you, Pearl, must remain a secret between us. Can you promise that?"

She looks put out. "You never have to ask me that," she says quietly. "You know I don't break confidences. Go on."

"Well, remember I told you I had a boyfriend back in Egypt?"

"Sarfraz," she says, a touch of disapproval in her voice.

"Well, I heard from him, and he says he misses me and wants me to come back to Egypt to be with him."

Pearl's face forms a mask as she stays silent, waiting.

"When I answered, I asked him if he had any way of helping track down where my father is."

"Because Sarfraz has joined an extremist group?" she asks dryly.

"Maybe," I say, though she knows I'm not stupid. "Anyway, today he told me he has learned where my father is being kept, and that he can help him escape."

Pearl leans forward and grabs my palms in hers. "This is information you need to give the police, immediately," she urges. "You don't really know who you are dealing with. Even if this boy knows where your father is, you know he doesn't have the power to set him free."

"We don't know that," I snap, then promptly add, "Sorry,

Pearl. But don't you see? The US government and my dad's company aren't getting anywhere. So maybe we have to trust that Sarfraz has different kinds of connections. And if he loves me, maybe he will break Dad out."

"Loves you?" Pearl's voice has gone cold, and I suddenly realize it was a bad idea coming over here.

"Okay, okay, I get why you're skeptical. You've never met Sarfraz. You don't know anything about our history. And I don't blame you for resenting my being confused about Karam. But leaving that aside for a sec, I want to tell you something else. There's this other guy who has been trying to contact me on the internet."

Pearl raises an eyebrow.

"He calls himself True Caliph, and he might be trying to radicalize me—"

Pearl's mouth falls open. "Don't ever answer such messages, Bronte! And you must report them to the imam, and to Sheriff MacDonald, and to—"

"Can I just finish what I was saying, Pearl?"

"Okay." Her lips draw into a tight line.

"He has offered to buy me two plane tickets. No strings attached. To fly to the Middle East to try and find my dad. We've been messaging back and forth, even though I know I shouldn't have answered him. He obviously feels sorry for me about my dad. But two free flights, Pearl: for me, and whoever else I want to bring with me. Two flights, and I can ask him to book as soon as I want."

"He'll have someone on the other end to meet you, kidnap you, and take you across a border, where you'll be forced to—"

"That may be what he thinks, but I'm not so dumb," I insist. "I've got Sarfraz to pick me up, and Sarfraz says he'll have my dad free by then. And even if he doesn't, well, I'll be there to help the Embassy or whatever, and be with Sarfraz."

Pearl's pretty oval face projects horror. "Why are you telling me this, knowing I'd never let you endanger yourself? Besides, your mom is never going to agree to go with you."

"I'm not inviting her, or telling her. She wouldn't approve. She never even knew about Sarfraz. I'll leave her a note explaining. She'll be happy I'm bringing Dad back. I want you to come, because you're my best friend. My only friend since I started dating Karam. You once said you've always dreamed of visiting Egypt. I thought maybe you'd see that it made sense and come with me."

"Come with you? Now you're crazy, Bronte. Me, who you always call Miss Unadventurous, getting on a plane without my parents' permission, to be with you on a suicide mission paid for by an enemy of Allah? I understand you're upset over your father's disappearance, Bronte, but if you're even vaguely considering this, I have another suggestion."

"Another suggestion," I echo, devastated she's being so negative, though not about to back down from doing whatever I have to do.

"You believe Karam is a recruiter, don't you?"

I hang my head. "I don't know what to believe," I lie, "but we found those pages—"

"—which mean nothing on their own"

"—and he hasn't returned any of my messages." Well, true till a short while ago.

"There's one sure way to find out if he is," she says, sitting erect in her desk chair, Aladdin's flying carpet backdropping her head.

I wait.

"Text him that you've decided to join an extremist group

in order to get to Yemen and find your father, and that you have an online recruiter ready to send you, unless he, Karam, wants to be your recruiter. If he's really a recruiter, he'll get you the money you need to fly over, find your dad, and be with Sarfraz, who is obviously a better man for you, if Karam has been lying and radicalizing people." The last line comes out a bit mocking, though I don't believe Pearl is capable of mocking.

"What?" I'm chewing on my lip, astonished that Pearl Saif, the purest Muslim I know—someone who'd pretty much do anything to prevent anyone getting radicalized— would come up with that advice. And that it actually makes sense.

"Uh-huh," I say. "And if he says no way, or doesn't answer?"

"Then come talk to me again before you answer this other guy. Promise?"

"Sisters don't need to promise, I'm told," I say with a weak smile. "Later, Pearl."

"Later, Bronte."

CHAPTER NINETEEN

It has been three days since Karam disappeared, and two since my father got kidnapped. Given how Mom's beyond comforting and it's super stuffy in our house, I'm twitching to get some fresh air. Mom's napping. Time to break out for some exercise. I lace up my running shoes and step out the door.

As I jog slowly up the west butte, my mind is on getting myself to Egypt to meet up with Sarfraz and search for Dad. I hope this walk will help me figure out how to word a reply to True Caliph, and to Karam and his news about Jaleela.

When I reach the top of the rise, I slump down on the bench. The very bench where I made out with Karam a few days ago.

I watch a turkey vulture circle high above. When I lower my eyes, I glimpse someone working his way up the opposite butte. The form is all too familiar. My butt freezes to the wood of the seat.

He's grinning as he does some aerial manoeuvres to break up his run on the steepening path, his back to the river and downtown. He cartwheels into a high dive, then does some butterfly twists: dips down, bends his knees, then launches off with legs and arms out and spinning as he rotates like a maniacally happy butterfly.

When he passes a little kid watching him with big eyes, Karam gives the boy a smile and thumb's-up. Then he's vaulting over every small boulder, railing, and stump in sight, working his way up the bluff. The higher he gets, the more fluid he becomes, springing exuberantly from one move to another, flying.

As he nears the top, not yet having spotted me, he breaks into an Arabic song.

"Didn't know you were a singer," I call out from across the chasm. My voice resembles the weather: dry and cold. "Thought you were in hiding."

He freezes like an escaped convict in prison searchlights. He's so near and yet so far: unreachable.

"Bronte," he calls out in a pained voice. "If only I could leap across."

"You seem pretty high-energy for someone who has been locked up in jail," I say, moving to the edge of the cliff on my side, fifteen feet across from where he stands with toes centred over his own precipice. "Maybe it's all the money you got from the girls you almost sent off to war? Or maybe it's the Paradise you're guaranteed for signing up soldiers of God?"

"Bronte, I'm still in hiding for reasons I can't explain. I just broke out for a little walk right now. I'm not who you think I am."

"I see. And who do I think you are?" I spit out.

Abruptly, he changes the subject. "How is your father?

Have they freed him yet? Are you and your mother doing okay?"

"Are you really buying me two plane tickets to go pick up my dad?" I demand, hands on my hips, eyes burning into him.

"Am I what? Where did that come from? I don't have any money, Bronte. You know that. If I did, and it would help you, I'd give you every cent I have. Is your dad actually free now?"

"No." I lower my hands from my hips, but keep my face hard. "It's pretty bad at school. The mosque is suffering too. And Pearl's not herself at all, sick with worry and praying for you all day long. Even the mosque-goers are praying for you."

His arms hang at his side.

"But there you are, practising parkour all gloriously cheerful on a bluff where no one can find you, including the reporters who've been harassing your family. Or is it your *ex*-family, now that you're in hiding?"

"Bronte, if I looked happy for a minute, it's because I was picturing Jaleela climbing the butte with me, bringing a picnic basket full of Yemeni treats for the three of us to share here. It'll happen for real when she's living in Richland, maybe with Pearl and my aunt and uncle sitting here, you and Jaleela and me waiting on a picnic blanket."

"I see. That's why you're so joy-joy."

He stares at me sorrowfully, studies me in from top to bottom. I'm dressed in blue jeans and an unzipped parka that reveals the same embroidered blouse I wore at Natalie's party, which seems like a decade ago.

"Bronte, stop it," he begs, glancing about as if to make sure no one is coming up behind either of us and overhearing our conversation. "I know how it looks, and I've stayed away to protect them, but—"

"But what, Karam?"

"I've been sworn to silence about what's going on. Which forces me not to explain anything, even to those I love." He looks at me meaningfully.

The pressure of my jaw eases a tiny bit, but I'm far from taken in. A boyfriend believed is a girlfriend naïve. No, girl, that doesn't even rhyme.

"Well, seeing as I've run into you, I have a request."

"To help find your father? I have no way to do that, Bronte. I'm sorry."

"No, to help me get to Yemen."

"What?"

"I've decided to sign up with an extremist group in order to get over there and search for my dad, and an online recruiter has offered me two free plane tickets. If you want me to go through you rather than him, this is your chance. Otherwise, I'm disappearing back down this hill, and I'll see you in Paradise, maybe."

His jaw drops. He stares hard at me, like he's trying to determine if this is a sick joke.

"It's over between us. You know that, right?" I continue, trying to ensure that a bolt of pain does not register in my voice.

He gazes at me with a morose look that I've never seen on him before. "I don't know that," he says bravely.

"I'm going to meet up with Sarfraz. He's helping me find my father."

"Your old flame is paying your way to Yemen? I thought he was in Egypt."

"He's not paying my way. The recruiter is. First I fly to

Egypt, then Sarfraz and I will make our way to where my father is."

"Bronte, you know any offer like that is a trap, and that Sarfraz is probably radicalized. Who's the second ticket for, anyway, your mom? You'd endanger her on this deluded idea of a mission?"

"I was hoping Pearl might go with me, but she turned me down. So I guess I'll just ask for one ticket and go by myself."

"By yourself?" His frantic-sounding voice cracks.

"I just asked you if you wanted to be my recruiter instead of the anonymous online one who has made me this generous offer. I'm waiting for your answer."

"All I want to do is jump over this gap and wrap you in my arms," he says.

My airways choke up, but only for a moment. "You have one more second to answer the question."

"Yes! Yes, I will be your recruiter. You'll be way safer with me than with him."

Tears spring to my eyes. *Wrong answer, Karam. It was a test, and you just failed.* But I say nothing, just whirl around and start down my hill, northwards towards my house and the school.

"I take it back, Bronte," he shouts. "Go with him, but let me be the person who flies with you."

I halt and turn around slowly, my cheeks wet with tears.

"Like I told you, Jaleela survived," he says, as if desperate to keep me from walking away. "She's in a refugee camp in Alexandria, just released from prison. But she's ill. I want to go to her. I'm willing to be your flying mate, if that's what it takes. You can still be with Sarfraz and go on to Yemen, if that's what you want."

My mouth opens and closes like an oxygen-starved fish. Then I'm struggling to look angry again.

"Are you or aren't you a recruiter, Karam? No lies."

He glances behind him once again for safekeeping. I find my eyes sweeping down my own empty hill. If he says no, his earlier comment—*yes, I will be your recruiter*—is a lie.

There's a long, painful pause.

"I am," he replies.

I bite my tongue. "But you'd fly on a competitor's ticket to go to your sister."

"Yes."

"And not because you think it'll get us back together, or that you can stop me from finding my dad?"

"Correct," he says, arms moving to his neck like there's a noose tightening around it.

"Then what should we do next?" I ask, unable to hide a quiver in my voice.

"Your contact will need my passport to book my flight. It's in my school locker." He gives me his lock combination. "Let's meet at the library at eight tomorrow night. Bring your laptop. And can you get my laptop from Pearl, please? It's on my desk at home."

I shift from one foot to the other. "Is this a trick, Karam? There aren't going to be police waiting to lynch me when I come to the library? You're not going to tell my mom?"

"You want to get to your dad. I want to get to Jaleela. We've both weighed the risks and are willing to take them, Bronte. And you've already pointed out that we're finished. All I ask is that we be together when you fill out whatever your recruiter asks you to in order to get those two tickets. I'm saying you should go through your guy, because I don't have the money for tickets. My recruits always pay for flights themselves."

My recruits. The words scald like hot oil going into my ears. So, he has said it. I look at him quizzically, trying to visualize the Karam I know, but not seeing him in the hunched figure across the gully from me.

"Eight o'clock," I repeat numbly, and turn to head down my hill.

CHAPTER TWENTY

At home, I slip in to see my mother sleeping on the sofa. Pulling a throw gently over her body, I kiss her forehead and tiptoe upstairs to my laptop.

It's like an electric shock lifts me right off my seat. My hands fly to my mouth to prevent a scream. An email from my father!

Dear Bronte:
I'm being allowed just this one email, and my orders are that it must go to you. I'm told this is a special favour being granted by an operative named Sarfraz. (I'm not aware of him, but he must be pretty high up in the operation, maybe even an emir.)
I am being kept in some kind of safe house here in Aden, and treated well. I have not been allowed to listen to any news or contact anyone, so I don't know how my case is playing out. I feel terrible for the pain and worry I am causing you and your mother, but I've also been told I am being smuggled into Alexandria, Egypt, tomorrow, and released by this Sarfraz

person shortly after that. I hope it is reliable information, as I don't want to give you false hope.

Please be patient and brave, as I know you will be, and as I must be too. I send you and Karen all my love and hope to be home safely with you soon.

Dad

He did it! He actually did it! My love for Sarfraz skyrockets into the stratosphere. If he's an emir, a commander, it means he's in way-deep on the terrorist thing. Even as I shiver with disgust at that, I feel a pinprick of pride for how his strength and daring has made him successful and recognized so quickly. If he can just retract all the extremist bullshit, I'll consider being with him. This is even an opportunity to introduce him to Dad.

Though I dare not admit it, I'm also overwhelmingly grateful that I will have a companion on the flight over. I feel safer flying with Karam. He won't let us get kidnapped or shot. He'll keep my nerves from fraying too much.

The next day is crazy long, me just waiting for eight p.m. I avoid Pearl at school. What would I tell her? Even just passing her in the hall, I fear she'll read my mind and do something to stop her cousin and me.

"Hey, it's the terrorist's girlfriend," some jerk calls out between classes.

"Ex-girlfriend," I level back at her, almost glad for the distraction and the chance to pretend I have no further contact with Karam.

"Good move. Can't blame you," the bitch says, suddenly friendlier.

"I heard he's in Richland Jail, maybe being waterboarded to give up his contacts," another girl offers, pausing to see whether that gets me riled.

"Deserves it," I play along.

"Seriously?" asks a male voice, and I twirl to see Dan staring at me. "You're one vindictive bitch, Bronte. Remind me not to get on your bad side. Or even your good side anymore." And he marches off.

Twenty shades of guilt pass through me, given that the last time I saw Dan I told him off for bullying Pearl and being so Islamophobic. Only a tiny percentage of Muslims are radicalized, I've told people so many times. Stop treating the rest like they're terrorists.

Yeah, well when you discover your boyfriend is one of them—a secret recruiter, even—who cares about tiny percentages? And he admitted it to me, the mega-liar-jerk!

So Karam and Sarfraz play for the same team. Damn both of them. But I'm in love with Sarfraz, who is freeing my dad because he loves me. Right?

I knock on Mr. Legendre's door during lunch break.

"Bronte! How are you?" he greets me with his usual broad smile.

I look up and down the hall and peer into the room to make sure no one's within hearing distance. "Fine, Mr. Legendre. Hey, I was just checking whether I could get Karam's laptop back. Like, now?"

"Of course! Oh wait, ah, no!" He clasps his hands together awkwardly. "It's at my house. Can I bring it in tomorrow?"

"Um, maybe you live nearby and have time to get it before school ends?"

"I don't, but I absolutely promise to bring it tomorrow. I

did find what, er, we were hoping for. I'll use it to finish the project tonight, okay?" He glances up and down the hall, too.

"No project," I say, frowning. "I just want the word." He'd better not snoop before I get it.

"Oh, sorry. Good you clarified. I'll let you do the navigating after you have the password, then. And I'll have that and the machine for you first thing tomorrow."

"Thanks," I say, sick with worry that Karam won't have it for tonight's meeting. Plus, the last thing I need is Mr. Legendre finding evidence that Karam is a recruiter and calling police on him. Well, that's what Karam deserves, I suppose, but it seems like he should get to see his sister first, and help her recover enough to come to Richland. Never mind get me safely to where I'm going. Shit, what warped logic I've acquired. Am I now an accomplice to an outlaw? To two outlaws! I need to change my taste in men.

"See you at parkour club, then," he says.

"Yes, see you there," I say distractedly, suffering belatedly from severe guilt for ever having stolen Karam's computer in the first place.

I wander into the library at seven-thirty, scouting for a private place to sit. Hardly anyone's here this time of night, just that same guy in a hooded sweatshirt bent over his laptop near the window, and the librarian loading books onto a trolley by the station. I choose a carousel desk well away from both, slip into it, and wait.

I hardly recognize him when he enters. He's wearing a balaclava under a hooded coat. He's in disguise, I realize, half amused. Still in hiding from the press, if not from the police.

"Hi," I say, as he plunks down beside me. I can't believe how my heart's ping-ponging. Am I really doing this? And Karam's really doing this?

"Where's my laptop?" he whispers, pulling off the balaclava.

"Couldn't get it. No one was home when I went over to your place. I'm really sorry. Can we do this without it?" I'm getting way too good at lying.

He pulls a laptop out of his backpack and switches it on. "Yeah, I borrowed this in case."

"Okay." Borrowed it from whom? Where's he hiding out? But I push all that from my mind, even as I become aware of the warmth and pleasant smell of his body just a foot away from me.

"When we're done, Bronte," he whispers, "you leave first. I'll leave ten minutes later. Wait for me, if you want me to walk you home."

"Okay," I say, acid chewing at my stomach lining. "Why are we using your computer?" I ask suspiciously.

"It's safer on my encrypted system," he says, half-glancing at the black-hooded guy in the corner, making me wonder if he's in on this somehow. Wasn't he here that night Karam was meeting with the fast-food girls? His hunched form even seems vaguely familiar. "But we will use yours in a minute to download the tickets. Trust me. I know what I'm doing."

I wonder, but I watch him bring up the internet, knowing my mom and dad would freak if they knew what I was doing.

"Here's the chatroom he uses to message me," I say, handing him a folded-up scrap of paper from my pocket.

"Good." Karam taps it into his address bar. "When he comes into the chatroom, I'll coach you how to reply to him."

"Or, um, you could just type in the answers for me?" I ask, wiping a moist hand on my T-shirt.

I'm relieved when he nods and positions his fingers over the keyboard. A ping makes us both jump.

"He's messaging!" I say, my stomach pitching like a boat in a storm.

"Perfect," Karam says all too calmly.

"Good afternoon, my jewel, Bronte. How are you today?" appears in the chat window.

I feel half dizzy, half nauseous.

"Excited and ready to join up!!!" Karam taps on the keyboard. I grit my teeth. How many times has Karam done this? Is that what he was doing for the fast-food girls that night I saw them in the library? Of course he was!

"Wonderful. You are my brave tigress," True Caliph responds, making my flesh prickle like insects are crawling over it. "You have told no one, correct?"

"Of course not!" Karam types, his fingertips flying over the keys. He eyes me to check my reaction. Just stare at the screen, I tell myself.

"Okay," types True Caliph. "I am sending the link for the application as we speak. Take your time. I'm right here if you have questions."

And so am I, you twisted pervert and murderer, preying on innocent young girls, I want to respond, but I stay mute, my nerves twisting with my guilt.

Seconds later, Karam has the form on the screen. "Ready to fill it in?" he whispers, pushing the laptop towards me.

I stare at the keys on his keyboard like they've been sprinkled with a poisonous powder.

"How about you read the questions to me and then type in the answers I give, but change them if what I say isn't okay?"

Karam nods. "I can do that as long as you keep your voice

very low and signal me if anyone comes near."

"Understood."

"First and last name," he begins. I watch him type them in.

"Blood type." His whisper is confident and steady.

"Why do they need to know that?" I ask sharply.

"In case you get injured," he replies smoothly.

"O negative."

"Nationality, marital status, height, weight, and eye colour—"

"They collect that intel to match female applicants up with fighter boyfriends, right?" I ask sarcastically.

"Yes," he replies without flinching.

"As if. More like they lock recruited girls up in a sex-slave warehouse for the fighters to rape every night after they return from a hard day of mass killing."

His face goes pale. But his tone is reassuring, caring. "Bronte, I'm not going to let anything bad happen to you. We're filling out this form so the two of us can get on a plane. You're not going all the way in this process. Just far enough to get the tickets that let us fly into Alexandria together."

I nod numbly.

"After we arrive, you can meet up with Sarfraz, who's going to rescue your father."

The cutting tone stings me like a scorpion. But who started this, anyway? I take a deep breath. "Okay, go on."

"How religious are you?"

"Not very," I say acidly.

"Previous military experience."

"None," I reply in a stony voice.

"Preferred role: fighter, suicide attacker, cook, first-aid attendant, or social media consultant."

I stare at him. He stares back. "Whatever," I mumble.

He clicks "social media consultant."

I cover my mouth to hide a giggle—I can't help it—and Karam's over-serious face finally creases into a smile. A beautiful one I wish would stay, and I wish were trustworthy. But it is not anymore.

"Press send when you're ready," he instructs.

Bravely, foolishly, numbly, I tap send.

"Done. Now we just have to wait for your recruiter to confirm he has received it."

I cringe at the words "your recruiter," and we wait in tense silence, not meeting one another's eyes.

"Bronte! That was quick," True Caliph purrs through the message window. "I'm so proud of you! Did you bring a photo to upload? Wearing your hijab, of course."

"Yes, LOL, wait just one minute!" Karam types. And uploads what I've given him.

"You are beautiful on the outside and inside," True Caliph responds a minute later. I imagine him leering at my face, and feel totally creeped out. "But it is your pure soul that I most admire." Demon-monster.

"Thank you, and praise be to Allah, whom I seek to serve," Karam types, frowning.

"You will, my gentle warrior, you will," my recruiter responds. "Now give me the information I need to supply you with two tickets to Alexandria, including passport details. Ten minutes after that, I will send the tickets to your preferred email address, okay?"

"Okay, thank you," Karam types, and supplies the requested information, including my email address.

The computer makes its funny, cartoon-type noise as True Menace signs off.

"We did it," I say flatly.

He shoves his computer to one side. I glance around. There's still no one around except the librarian and the geek on the other side, minding his own business.

"Okay, open up your laptop now, Bronte."

Hearing my name on Karam's lips makes me want to turn to him, kiss him, pretend nothing has come between us, and run away from all this. But it's too late now.

Congratulations, Bronte. Your flights are attached. A contact will make himself known to you as you arrive at the airport in Alexandria, Egypt, and will help you purchase visas there. May Allah bless your journey and our cause.

True Caliph

"Flight leaves tomorrow night," Karam says in a super-hushed and awed whisper, like he can't believe we've pulled this off. He takes down the information he needs. "Okay, close down your computer and walk away casually."

"See you at the airport," I whisper, reaching over and squeezing his hand. Then I'm up and fleeing before I can consider taking it further, and before he can respond. Anyway, he's busy reading a message from Jaleela on his email account, on his borrowed laptop.

"Bronte!" he suddenly calls out, but the library's front doors close behind me, and I pretend not to hear him. I turn towards my house. It's cool and dark out, the street lights offering small, insufficient pools of light beneath a weak moon. I walk super fast, because I need to get home, spend the evening with my mom, and write her a really nice goodbye note before tomorrow evening. And notify Sarfraz when my flight gets in.

CHAPTER TWENTY-ONE

Sarfraz! I need to believe he's the old Sarfraz, the daring traceur star who chose me above all the other parkour girls in the Academy. Sarfraz, who could make my skin sizzle with one look. Sarfraz, my secret habibi, who taught me moves that stirred my very soul—never mind increased my fluency at Arabic and parkour.

If he has gone to the Dark Side, I will resist and reject him. I won't be a terrorist's woman. But if he holds the key to putting my family back together again, I'll give him a chance, maybe convince him I'm worth turning his back on fundamentalist Islam for.

"Bronte." It's Mr. Noori, walking towards me with a squat, ugly bulldog on a leash. "On your way home? Please let me escort you. I never like to see young girls alone on the streets at night."

"It's not far to my house, Mr. Noori, thanks anyway."

"But I insist," he says.

I break into a run, in such a hurry to lose Scarface that I

fail to notice a van pull up alongside me, heading my direction. A window rolls down.

"Bronte. Are you okay? Need a ride?"

"Mr. Legendre." I glance back. Noori is coming this way, yanking on his dog's leash to catch up with me.

"Um, sure." I hop in.

"Doing homework at the library?"

"Yes." Not about to 'fess up to what I was really doing.

"Computer science, hopefully," he teases with that charming grin of his.

I smile. "Too much homework in eleventh grade," I complain. "Interferes with important stuff like parkour."

"Yes, but good grades will get you where you want to go. What are your plans after graduation? Do I remember you saying you want to start a parkour gym for kids? If you need any advice on that, I'd like to help you lead the life waiting for you."

Something about that sentence turns me quiet. Then my cell phone buzzes. I dig it out and read the text from Karam: "Jaleela's emails were false, phony! Maybe Sarfraz's & ur dad's 2?"

I have trouble taking that in. Wait. *I'd like to help you lead the life waiting for you.* A phrase True Caliph used!

If Jaleela's, Sarfraz's, and my dad's emails weren't real, it means someone has hacked both computers, Karam's and mine. Someone who knows how to steal passwords. Someone who wants us on a plane to the Middle East. Someone who could have taken my laptop from the parkour room cubbyhole and returned it to the wrong cubby an hour later. A recruiter.

The recruiter.

"Bronte? You've gone all quiet on me," Legendre says, slowing near my house.

"You're True Caliph? Not Noori?" I blurt out.

His head jerks my way, face draining of colour. My heart is pounding hard enough to break my ribcage. He eases off the brake and is now passing my house.

My phone buzzes again. "AW = Legendre." True Caliph is truly Mr. Legendre? Karam just figured that out? How?

I'm about to pull up the door handle and bail out of the van, when Legendre floors the pedal and we accelerate at warp speed.

"What are you talking about, Bronte, my sister?"

The words are innocent enough, but neither the tone nor the speed he's now driving convinces me I haven't hit bull's-eye. Hurtling along the road at breakneck speed, he narrowly misses hitting an oncoming black sports car I recognize as Dan's—Jazel and Vansh crunched up in front with the fast-car-loving Texan. Joyriding. Dan lays on the horn. Wish I was with them. Wish I could signal them. Wish I'd waited for Karam, maybe even Scarface, to walk me home.

Minutes later, Legendre veers off the main road, heading east now towards the western butte's unlit parking lot halfway up the butte. He tears around the corner onto the dirt road at near tipping speed.

I have my cell phone between my knees, desperately texting "SOS. Bench" to Karam, but then Legendre grabs it from me and tosses it out his window.

"Hold on, sister," he growls.

"Why?" I shout. "Why, after risking your life and losing your friends fighting terrorists in Afghanistan, would you become one?"

"Fool," he says. "Yes, I risked my life and lost almost

everyone in my battalion. And what did I get for that? What did we Muslim fighters get for that? Respect? No! Admiration? No! I returned to find that the French hate Muslims. They won't hire them, won't house them, won't look at them without fear and loathing. Even if we're vets." He spits out his window. "So I turned my back on the bastards and became what they assumed I was anyway. I discovered a new, more glorified path, and I thank Allah for it every day."

Stomach lurching, I'm speechless as I'm slammed back and forth from van door to stick shift, only my seatbelt saving me from serious bruising. He thinks he's going too fast for me to dare open the door and jump but he forgets I'm a star traceuse who knows exactly how to tumble.

I release the seatbelt, and with a quick, vicious yank on the handle, fly out of the moving vehicle. The moment my feet hit the ground, I reach my hands downward and tuck into the fastest shoulder roll of my life. The momentum from the roll launches me to my feet. Hearing the screech of his brakes and his door slamming, I race up the slope—barbed-wire fencing preventing a downhill run, and Legendre behind me.

"You can't outrun me, infidel!" he shouts. "You're not even going to live to the top of this hill."

He's way stronger and fitter than me, and I'm scared shit-less, but I try to convince myself otherwise. Keep yakking, you scum bucket, I think as I vault over boulders, jump, and climb swiftly to the top of a cliff face. Use up your lungs with angry words, you reprobate. All this time I trusted him, admired him. Idiot-wrapped-in-a-moron me! He cleverly made nice with Imam Taha, who never suspected a spy and radicalizer in his midst.

And who handed him Karam's laptop on a silver platter?

I'm the mother of all lunkheads. A boyfriend untrusted is a boyfriend busted. Lame, Bronte. Just keep running. He's fast, and he's gaining, but you're not meant to die tonight.

I cut through some brush, hoping to lose him off-trail. Low bushes prove no obstacle to me as I whip through the park. It sounds like he's on the trail I've left behind. I jump towards a log, clearing it with a push from one hand. The moment I'm airborne, I hear Legendre bashing through the bush about thirty feet behind. As I make a split-second decision to head towards another trail, I hear him land out of his vault over the log. He's gaining.

I waste no time. The trail turns a sharp corner at the base of a steep bank by an outhouse. Rather than risk a slide on the gravel path at this speed, I tic-tac against the wall of the outhouse to redirect myself. As I make the turn, I glance over my shoulder to see Legendre emerge onto the trail only fifteen feet behind. I have to put more space and obstacles between us, but it's too risky to do anything very technical. If I mess up, he's got me.

Ahead I see a bear-proof trash bin next to a chain-link fence. Yes! I kong up to the angled surface of the dumpster to vault the fence. Hopefully Legendre will hit it less smoothly. But mounting the trash container, I slip on a coating of fine dust while leaping to the fence. Teeth gritted, I barely manage to get a hand and foot to the top of the cold metal and vault past it. Not as fast as I'd hoped.

He's less than two lunges behind me by the time I reach the bench, the one from which I called out nasty things to Karam the other day. Even before he told me he was a recruiter. Which was probably a lie.

An accusation I lobbed at him awhile back, double-kongs itself into my brain: *The Coast Guard illegally took you across the international line to ships they knew were run by people smugglers? Not likely. Not for free.*

Not for free, indeed. Someone must have made him play teen recruiter in a sting operation as a condition for getting free. That's my guess now, and if I'm right, it's why he used those girls. That's why he couldn't tell me anything. If I'm "Part II" of the exercise, a decoy recruit, and Legendre now knows it, our computer science teacher no longer wants us on a plane. He wants us dead. Tonight. Why didn't I keep my big mouth shut?

"Devil!" he's screaming. "I've got you now! Think I don't know how to twist the necks of infidels like you? I'm an f-ing killing machine when Allah deems it necessary."

He has cornered me on the cliff's edge, it's true. And the gap to the other side is too far to jump. But thanks to Vansh, there's one move I have that my old-school coach probably doesn't: the polecat. And there's a bare stretch of red maple trunk nine feet away, itching to feel my shoes on it. Getting from there to the cliff on the other side will be dicey, but I'd rather die falling than by strangulation.

I feel a whoosh of air behind me, Legendre leaping from the bench, expecting to take me down. That's when I jump off of one leg and raise the other, foot turned outward, to catch the tree trunk like it's a gym-room pole. His grasping hands, I presume, close around air as his body makes a thud landing in the dirt near the edge of the cliff. I make sure my running shoes plant themselves on the tree just behind the balls of the feet. Only then do I grab the rough bark with both hands, squatting into this convenient maple until my arms are fully extended. Doing it perfectly keeps me from slipping, keeps me alive. But I'm not done yet.

"Bronte!"

A figure appears six feet away on the far bluff. It's almost too dark to see him, but I'd know Karam's voice anywhere.

As his shadow seems to dive off the bluff, I scream, but then, even in the murky night, I get that he is now hanging off the side of the opposite cliff to give me a target to jump to.

"Bronte!" shouts another voice on the cliff top above Karam: Vansh's. "You can do it. Just turn and do a cat-180. Pivot your hips as you jump back and turn to latch onto Karam. Got it? Jump, look, turn, and catch!"

"Bronte! We're all with you!" comes Jazz's excitable voice.

"Show us how it's done," commands Dan.

What are they all doing here in the dark? I wonder, my heart soaring beyond my fear. Karam must've joined their joyride and hijacked them to respond to my SOS. Of course: the road up to the eastern bluff ends much higher up than the one for the western bluff, so they figured they'd use it to reach the gap in time.

I glance over to memorize the location of Karam's shadowy body, then jump with every well-trained muscle primed, like we've practised so many times. In mid-air I'm turning as if Vansh's guiding hands are on me. I catch onto Karam's hips, landing my feet against the cliff face below him while praying to God, Allah, and whoever else might be looking out for us, that I don't pull Karam off the precipice. Little do I know that Vansh and Dan are holding onto him from above, ready to yank us both up like trophy fish.

I've barely vacated the tree trunk when I hear Legendre's body brush it. And even as I'm hauled up onto the top of the east butte by my chain of saviours, I hear his harrowing cry as he plummets into the ravine.

CHAPTER TWENTY-TWO

Disentangling myself from the pile of bodies, adrenalin pumping on overtime, I pivot in the weak moonlight and fling myself back to the tree with a reckless, second well-timed polecat. Then I down-climb the tree like a firefighter on a pole, heedless of the scratches to my body, and knowing none of my clubmates are likely to risk their lives to follow me.

"What're you doing?" Vansh calls out.

"Checking to see if he's alive. I'm the first-aider, remember?"

I land lightly beside our instructor, whose twisted form resembles a chalk-outlined figure at a murder scene. There's blood on his forehead, and he's silent. I adjust his head to ensure an airway.

"He's breathing. Probably concussed," I mumble. "Gotta call 911."

The fist shoots up from nowhere and connects like a rock with my Adam's apple. It sends my head skyward, like it's going to rip right off my neck. Stars sprinkle down from the black sky.

I scramble backwards and try to shout for help, but only a raspy croak comes out of my throat.

"You're dead, kafir"—unbeliever—he pronounces as he crawls towards me, one misshapen leg dragging.

"You mimicked my father, you bastard," I respond in a hoarse whisper. "You pretended to be Karam's sister and Sarfraz. You stole our passwords, and Allah only knows how many kids you've sent to their deaths overseas."

"Martyrs," he corrects me, scrabbling forward with a beastly glint in his eye. "I made them honourable fighters with a cause, to battle disbelievers. And you? Nothing but a hypocrite who has been dating Karam, the devil himself. His sister Jaleela is dead, gone. Drowned because his family tried to flee a holy fight they could have let Karam join. And when he survived, he chose to live among depraved heathens like you—and worse, plot against us."

Mr. Legendre continues to shuffle forward on his elbows, dragging a limp leg. The blood on his forehead has run down to drip off his beard.

"Depraved is what you are," I say, struggling to get my wind back and measuring the distance to the red maple. "You follow a false Islam that promotes murdering innocent people. You're the reason the West hates law-abiding Muslims like Karam and Pearl. Asswipe."

"Tut, tut. Language, Bronte. But you've never been a nice Christian girl, have you? Pretending to convert to Islam so you can seduce an Islamic refugee. I don't know who your Yemeni boyfriend has been working for, but it's all over now, slut. Burn in hell."

I shoulder-roll away and claw the dirt to escape, but he

catches my ankles and drags me back. My knee aims for his privates, but he's too fast for me, injured or not. He's also twice my size and a solid mass of muscle. Next thing I know, I'm on my back and he's straddling me. Both his hands close around my already bruised throat. I make one squeaky sound that can't possibly carry to the top of the ravine, before I'm speechless, unable to breathe, kicking and punching and trying to break the hold.

His fist punches me hard in the face. I hear my nose crack, and a blinding light followed by agonizing darkness fills one eye socket. Pain and panic are all I have left, as I twist and jerk in an effort to dislodge him before I black out.

Be strong to be useful, rings in my head. *Etre fort pour être utile.* In one final effort, I plant my feet on the ground and thrust my hips up as hard as I can. The palm on my throat releases itself as Legendre catapults over my head.

Then hands are pulling at both of us, rolling my attacker onto his face, and grinding him into the ground. I hear voices: Karam's, Vansh's, Dan's, and Jazel's. Something is bucking beneath them, but they seem to have it under control.

"Always wanted to beat me up a Muslim." Dan's voice. "One of the tiny percentage that are extremist, I mean."

"Call 911," I mutter, a headache engulfing me. Did they all polecat over to the tree and come down it? Just because I was foolish enough to do so? They must have, beautiful idiots that they are!

"No need," Karam says, cupping his hands under my neck and leaning down to kiss me lightly on the lips.

Sirens sound from the riverside road at the head of the ravine a quarter of a mile away. There are police-cruiser headlights and flashing red lights, but it's the portable search-lights that all but blind us as Sheriff MacDonald comes galloping our way over the rough ground, officers at his heel. Something about his silhouetted body makes me squint with my one good eye and think hard. Sheriff MacDonald: that was the black-hooded figure skulking in the library. Was he part of Karam's sting operation all along?

The sheriff clamps handcuffs on Legendre and ignores the spew of nasty-sounding French words coming out of our teacher's mouth.

"Clear the way for the ambulance crew and stretchers," I hear him order. "Bronte, are you okay?"

"I'm good," I say hoarsely.

Imam Taha kneels beside me. "You escaped Mr. Noori, who I put there to protect you, Bronte. But we're all here with you now."

"Thank you, Imam Taha," I say, totally appreciating his soothing presence.

I stare at the night sky and wonder if it's the same sky my father is under in Yemen. Families that reunite will soon be alright. Nice one, girl.

CHAPTER TWENTY-THREE

"So, just as Bronte was leaving the library, you got an email from Jaleela?" Imam Taha is asking Karam, as he, the sheriff, Mr. Noori, and I sit around a table at Bubba's Burgers.

I touch my bandaged eye, wince, and turn my head to take in everyone.

"Yes," says Karam. "When I replied earlier to her email, I asked her what part of Aden would always be with her, and she replied, 'All of it.'"

Noori scratches his head. Sheriff MacDonald and I, who know the story already, are bemused and impatient.

"I don't understand," the imam says.

"I asked her that because I knew if it was really her, she'd say her dimples. You see, the city is built in a crater, and Father and I always teased her that her dimples resembled that crater. When I got her email, I knew immediately it wasn't really her—that someone had gotten hold of my email account and was posing as my sister."

I smile again at his cleverness.

"I see," says Imam Taha thoughtfully.

"And if someone was pretending to be my sister, they could easily have hijacked information on Bronte's computer and be mimicking her father and Sarfraz too. So I texted that concern to Bronte. It still hurts that I allowed my need to believe it was really Jaleela to put Bronte and me in danger."

"And this posing as people he found in your email messages was in order to win Bronte over as a fighter," Noori says in a low voice, shaking his head and clenching his fists. "Why did I never suspect Legendre? Not even for a moment!"

"Because he's smooth and professional," I reply bitterly. "And he clinched the deal by offering us free flights to where we both wanted to go, thanks to emails he generated that made us *want* to go."

"Tickets Karam collected on Bronte's laptop, so I wouldn't know about that part of the deal," the sheriff says, eyes narrowed at us. "I was privy to everything else he was doing on our linked-up computers as I sat well away from them in the library that night. Using another computer was not part of our agreement at all. Not that Karam or I would ever have let you get on that plane, at least if we were still following Plan A. We just wanted to catch your recruiter."

Karam turns to me. "If the sheriff had known about the free flights, he'd have stopped us for sure."

"Damn right, son, and for good reason. But go ahead and tell the rest of your story," the sheriff says.

"When I was still in the library, as soon as I texted Bronte about Jaleela, I jumped up to run out and catch her," Karam continues, "but as I was heading for the library door—"

"—I shouted to Karam, 'It's Legendre!'" the sheriff says

triumphantly. "I'd hit pay dirt on my computer. I'd finally identified our evil recruiter!"

"Of course, I figured I'd better get that info to Bronte too," Karam says ruefully. "As I stepped outside, I saw Mr. Noori walking his dog, and he was all agitated, telling me about how Bronte had just gotten away from him—"

"I was there for a reason: under Imam Taha's orders to protect her," Noori explains. "Though he did not share why."

"So," Karam continues, "Bronte had climbed into Legendre's van, but there was Dan cruising down the street in his fast car with half the parkour club, coming in the opposite direction."

"You could have—should have—come back inside the library and informed me what was up. We could've chased Bronte and Legendre in my cruiser," the sheriff says with a frown.

"Instead I flagged down Dan, hopped in, and texted Bronte that True Caliph was actually Legendre. I was horrified when I got her SOS in response. And then there's Jazz bouncing around in her seat, saying that after they'd passed Legendre and Bronte, she'd looked back and seen them speeding into the park's west entrance. I decided the east entrance was our only chance of getting near the bench in time—the road that side goes almost all the way to the top— so I deputized Dan to get us up there fast. Did he ever! He drives like a NASCAR champ, turns out. As we held on for our lives, I texted the sheriff."

"You knew she'd try the leap across?" Imam Taha asks incredulously.

"Either that or I would," Karam says soberly. "As it turns out, we all did the tree jump, with Vansh's coaching, after she leaped back to the tree and climbed down it to check whether Legendre was dead.

"Meanwhile, the sheriff alerted me," Imam Taha interjects. "I was aware of Karam's activities from the time Pearl brought me the printout. That's when I called Sheriff MacDonald and he explained it all to me, swearing me to secrecy until the operation was finished. I gave it my approval at that time, although it was very difficult keeping information from Pearl's family," he adds, frowning.

"What I don't understand," Noori says, stroking his beard and looking at me, "is how Legendre got hold of both your computers in the first place."

I sigh, fish an ice cube out of my glass of cola, and pop it inside the bandage covering my damaged eye. The eye still hurts like hell, but will do a full recovery, according to the doctors who treated me at Richland Hospital. The nose broke but will fix on its own.

"He took mine from a cubbyhole at parkour club while I was working out," I explain, "and used his password-cracking software capability to get what he needed. I noticed it was in a different place after the workout, but didn't think anything more about it."

"And he did the same with Karam's?" Imam Taha asks.

I tug at a thread on my sweater, not wanting to admit my part in that. But if I don't say it, the sheriff probably will.

"After the news linked the two sisters and Karam, Pearl and I went snooping in Karam's desk drawer. We were shocked to find a printout of recruiters' guidelines."

"I should never have printed them out," Karam says in an agonized voice. "They're what Captain Hussein sent me. Remember when I told you about my family drowning off Alexandria, and me getting dumped on Nelson's Island?"

"Of course."

"After I'd spent a couple of cold, scary hours waiting there, a vessel pulled up."

"The Coast Guard."

"Yes. I tried to hide under a boulder, but the officers landed with dogs who sniffed us all out. We were ushered on board by the captain." His voice cracks.

I lean forward to make sure I hear every word.

"It was Captain Hussein of the Egyptian Coast Guard, also an undercover operative for Mukhabarat, the Egyptian intelligence agency collaborating with the CIA. He demanded our passports and destinations. I had to tear off my chest packet to surrender mine. He grilled me for my story, and I told him the name of the ship I was supposed to board. I was in an agitated state, having just lost my family and fearing I was about to be killed or thrown in prison."

I nod sympathetically.

"He arrested the other people on the island with me, but said he'd deliver me to the ship my family had booked, in time, on one condition."

Karam pauses and swallows several times.

"Go on," I encourage him, though by now we all pretty much know the condition.

"That I'd go through the motions of signing up three teen fighters for an extremist cause."

I hear deep resentment in Karam's voice even now, and shudder at the scenario.

"Hussein promised me that none of my recruits would actually join up or be hurt, because it was a sting operation to catch recruiters targeting young people. He hooked me up with a CIA guy, 'Agent RL,' here in Richland, who turned out to be Sheriff MacDonald."

The sheriff offers a tight smile. Retiring from the CIA now that his cover is blown, I figure.

"RL. That's who you kept getting calls from on your phone, and messages that made you guard your laptop? Maybe he was the person who asked you to hold a session on Islam? And who I heard you talking to once when—"

"Yes."

"You could easily have broken your promise to Hussein at any time," Sheriff MacDonald says gently. "Neither Hussein nor I have ever had any hold over you."

"But when I make a promise, I carry through," Karam says resignedly.

"Why didn't Hussein just have *you* sign up in order to trap a recruiter?" I ask.

"Naturally, we thought of that from the start," the sheriff says, "but Karam couldn't have been the first one, or we'd never have had more than one. We needed him to run that seminar on Islam, in case it picked up some candidates, which it did. But when he showed up at the station during the media circus, the girls exposed him—made him a suspect. We feared the real recruiter might be wary of Karam. So he was a no-go as the third recruit."

"And then I volunteered," I say, cringing.

"You were the perfect candidate," Sheriff MacDonald says as Noori shakes his head again, "understandably high on Legendre's wishlist. Nonreligious, Arabic-speaking, parents split, and playing at Islam."

"How dare you!" Noori bursts out as the imam leans forward, face also a study in restrained fury.

"I apologize," the sheriff says quickly, meekly.

"Plus blond, female, and fit," I finish for him with a

generous helping of sarcasm. "What's not for a recruiter to like?"

"When I first asked Karam to approach you, he refused," the sheriff tells me. "He didn't want to involve you or put you in danger. And later, he couldn't fathom how your father's disappearance would influence you to join the kind of extremists who probably kidnapped him."

I look at Karam appreciatively, then turn my attention back to the sheriff.

"I told Karam that if you believed he could help you find your father, he could use his pull with you to get you to fill out a form. As a favour to him, since by then you believed he was a recruiter anyway."

"I refused to do it, telling him I wasn't lying to you anymore,'" Karam speaks up.

"So I backed off. I apologized and admitted I was just grasping at straws," the sheriff finishes.

"But then you showed up on the bluff suggesting it yourself." Karam turns to me, shaking his head like he's amazed at that still.

"I did," I say ruefully, not about to tell him it was Pearl's idea as a way of testing him. "Anyway, backing up to my story, after we found the recruiter guidelines in Karam's desk drawer, I was so panicked that I nabbed his laptop, too. When I couldn't figure out his password, I handed it to Legendre, whom I trusted, to do it. I feel really, really badly about that."

"And I've forgiven her," Karam says.

"Allah is all-forgiving and urges us to be the same," says Imam Taha.

"But Legendre using what he found on your laptops to impersonate a deceased loved one and others, all to lure you

to evil is unforgiveable," Noori dares to say. "You two would
have been kidnapped the second you stepped off the plane,
you know. May Legendre rot in prison," he adds, ignoring the
frown and sharp look that evokes from Imam Taha.

I sigh but resist leaning into Karam in the imam's
presence.

"Oh, Karam! I meant to tell you!" the sheriff says. "I
received an email from Hussein right before I got here. Want
me to read it to you?"

"Go for it," Karam says tiredly.

Dear RL:
A hearty congratulations on wrapping up the Richland case
and detaining a wanted recruiter who specialized in preying
on teens.
I knew when I met Karam that the boy was worth freeing,
and that he'd keep his word. I'm pleased to hear he has
settled into his new life, but should he ever return to the
Middle East, let him know I can arrange employment
for him.
Warmly,
Hussein

"Thanks for that," Karam says. His lets his head fall back
like he's relieved he no longer has to deal with the Coast
Guard captain.

I drop another ice cube into my now-soaked bandage and
picture Karam shivering and desperate on Nelson's Island in
Alexandria's Abū Qīr Bay. He's lucky Hussein wasn't the
other kind of double agent, pressing boys into service as
fighters rather than spies. I'm lucky, too. I'd never have met
Karam if it weren't for the Egyptian Coast Guard. How

different his life would be right now if this Hussein hadn't taken a chance on him. I guess the guy was a "nice Coast Guard officer" after all, even if manipulative.

"How are Caitlin and Chloe?" I ask the sheriff, prompting Karam to bite his lip.

"I made sure they got off pretty easy," he says. "They're doing community service hours to fulfill the judge's orders."

"What kind of community service?" I ask, curious.

"One's doing social media work for our new anti-radicalization campaign aimed at youth, and the other is reading to residents at an old folks' home."

I smile as I rub my bruised neck. "Better in Richland than in the Middle East."

"Karam, you're back at your aunt's and uncle's now?" Imam Taha asks.

"I am," Karam says, "though I'm grateful to you and your wife, Sheriff MacDonald, for the hospitality while things were a little crazy. Aunt Reem and Uncle Lando said they never doubted me for a minute, and Uncle Lando claims he enjoyed chasing the media off. Pearl—well, she took a lot of flak but never flinched, and never doubted me either. I owe them so much."

Imam Taha smiles. He should smile more often, I think.

"You and your mother are in touch with your father again?" the sheriff addresses me. "I understand the kidnappers have announced a release date."

"In shaa Allah," I respond.

"I guess that means you'll soon be back at the mosque?" Imam Taha asks me, his long fingers steepled in front of him.

"Maybe ready to get more involved with the sisters in the youth group?" Noori lays it on.

"How about I get past this eye pain and then decide?" I say.

"I forgot my wallet," says Karam. "Would anyone be willing to order me a Bubba's burger? I'm starving."

That makes Ryker and Tommy look our way as they breeze through the café's door.

"Hey, it's Bronty-Sore-Ass and Pow-Wham-Kazam!" Tommy says, "parkour club undercover spies and heroes, who pound evil teachers in the dead of night. I'll buy you a burger, bro! Double-decker with pickle's your fave, right?"

"One for Bronte too?" Ryker adds. "No starving one-eyed pirate traceuses in this joint. And are we ever pissed about missing the action the other night!"

I chuckle at the one-eyed pirate bit, but Karam's face turns color as the imam and caretaker study him.

"You must mean the veggie burger with pickle," Imam Taha says. "They don't serve halal meat here."

"Yes, sir. That's exactly what I meant!" Tommy replies, winking at Karam, then turning to the server. "One double-decker veggie with pickle, please. Plus three double-decker regulars, two with extra fries and one with onion rings. Hey, when the heck are you guys gonna get halal burgers on the menu, anyway? They're the latest rage at Three Rivers High School."

"I did not know that," says the manager, standing behind the server and casting his eyes around our group. "I'll look into that, pronto."

CHAPTER TWENTY-FOUR

"Dad!" I scream as his face comes on the screen. Mom and I are huddled around the kitchen table with Mom's laptop in front of us. It's the first time we've seen him in all the harrowing weeks since he was kidnapped. His face looks thin and haggard, but the familiar smile is the most welcome sight in the world.

"Where are you? How are you?" Mom asks him, tears rolling down her cheeks already.

"I've been treated well," he says in a tone that doesn't convince me. "I was handed over to American Embassy personnel this morning." He sounds tired, but relieved. Mom and I squeeze hands.

"How's Richland? How are you holding up, Karen and Bronte?"

I let Mom talk for a while, happy just to drink in the view of my father in real time.

"How's your parkour?" he asks me eventually, as if casting around for a safe topic.

"I've got some new moves, and a few bruises from

learning them," I say lightly—and truthfully. Bruises from Legendre's crazy ride up the hill, bruises from the van escape and tree moves that saved my skin, and more from descending the tree and getting pummelled by "my recruiter" aka computer science teacher. I shudder at the memory of that night, and berate myself once again for the maniacal stupidity of believing those emails were from Sarfraz and Dad, and for acting as recklessly as I did. Mom's still not over the shock and horror of my arranging to board a plane back to the Middle East, and then nearly getting killed on the butte. Her freak-out was epic. She went ape-shit-squared and I deserve being grounded forever.

"Sounds good. What are the names of these new moves?" Dad asks while sipping from a water bottle.

"A polecat and cat-180 combo," I report.

"Aha. Ensuring your nine lives," he tries to joke.

"Got that right. She'll tell you all about it next week," my mother inserts, narrowing her eyes meaningfully at me before turning back to the screen. "I can't wait to see you, dear. You have no idea how we've worried."

"I'm sorry," he mumbles, stroking some chin stubble absent-mindedly. "When I get home, how about I take some time off? We'll spend some family time together. Maybe go camping or something."

"That would be awesome, Dad!"

"Exactly what we need," Mom says, eyes leaking again.

Dad chats some more, giving sketchy details of the turnover and informing us that he cannot divulge details.

We update him on new construction projects in town, the school's search for a new computer science teacher, and an expanded menu at Bubba's Burgers.

"I'm being signalled that my time is up," he breaks in

with an apologetic voice. "But next time we speak, it'll be in person. I love you both. I hope you know how very much."

It's waterworks around the kitchen table as we say our goodbyes. Finally he disappears, and Mom and I lift our fingers to linger on the blank screen at the same time, then smile warmly at one another.

"He'll be here soon," Mom says, "and everything will be alright. We won't tell him about your escapade—your lapse of judgment that was the near death of me—till he's settled. And you've promised me, dear, absolutely promised me, you'll never ever pull anything like that again. No more sneaking around. And Dad and I will get to meet this Karam next week."

"No more sneaking around, and you'll like him, Mom."

"He makes you happy," she says, pulling me close. "Of course we'll like him."

CHAPTER TWENTY-FIVE

We meet outside at the community centre at our usual parkour club time, but with no parkour instructor having replaced Legendre yet, we've opted to do a run today, working in some parkour en route.

"Hi, everyone," Pearl says shyly, as she rounds the corner of the building. She's wearing brand-new electric-green running shoes, loose trousers and shirt, and a tightly pinned hijab. "Can I join you? I've decided I need to get out more. I might even try parkour, if you'll let me."

"Pearl!" Karam and I both rush forward and lift her off her feet in a rush to embrace her.

"It's about time!" I say. "And you absolutely do need to get out more!"

"Welcome," say the others, though Natalie and Dan hang back a little.

"Seems weird to do parkour outside in public," Tommy says, as we stretch our calves and run in place to warm up. Pearl beams as she copies our movements.

"Doing parkour on the run is what we did all the time in

Aden. It's full of memories for me," Karam replies, as we peel away towards the river.

"Love the fresh air!" Jazel enthuses, her red hair flying as she grabs my hand and pulls me into a sprint that sets us off giggling.

"It's what stuntmen do in the movies," Vansh declares as he strides to a park bench and leaps from arm-rest to arm-rest. "No one has ever outdone Sebastien Foucan's *Casino Royale* chase scene," he enthuses. "Jumping from a high crane to a high crane? Wow!" His eyes sparkle as he pop-vaults up onto a seven-foot-high park wall, then drops down to a precision landing on a low garden ledge, as if recreating Foucan's stunt.

Pearl speaks up. "Yeah, but parkour isn't just about extreme chase scenes. I understand there's philosophy behind it."

"True," Natalie says, "but Vansh, when you do get a job in Hollywood, you will help me get on a film crew, right?"

"Why not?" Vansh replies with a chuckle, sprinting into a jump at a tall fencepost to perform his now well-polished polecat.

"Karam and Pearl, I owe you apologies for the way I acted my first few months here," Dan says, starting to puff as we round a river bend. "Wasn't till I talked to a minister that I kinda got my head screwed on right about Islamists and all that. After Bronte made me. Oh, and Karam, I s'pose I should thank you for the save when I was trying the polecat that day in the gym." He pulls his ball cap low.

Karam slaps him on the back. "Water under the bridge, friend."

"Tell me sometime what the minister said," Pearl says in a small voice, but her smile is big.

"Sure," Dan says shyly.

"I'm sorry about the social media stuff," Natalie mumbles, looking at me rather than Karam, and then quickly away.

"Apology accepted," I say a little stiffly, not yet able to forgive her for what she posted.

"How come we're not heading up the bluff, Brontosaurus?" Tommy asks me in a slightly winded voice as he does a feeble tic-tac on a nearby boulder.

"We're headed for a certain red maple tree," I reply, launching into a series of jumps across a row of broad wooden bollards that the others, minus Pearl, soon mimic.

For the next ten minutes, we're a tag team of virtuoso traceurs and traceuses, running, jumping, and vaulting our way along the river. Karam's at my side all the way, his chestnut eyes sparkling.

"Do you know that you have ocean eyes and desert hair?" he whispers.

"Wow, you should be a Hollywood scriptwriter. So, what was your password, anyway?"

"If I told you that, I'd have to kill you."

"No you wouldn't. You'd just have to change it."

"True. Okay, it was 'dimples.'" He reaches out to touch mine. I smile and reach for his hand.

"Traceurs who play together, stay together," I declare.

"I hope so."

We warm the winter desert with our sweat, tame the twisted trail with our tread, and send tumbleweeds rolling with our passing. Pearl contributes by singing an Arab pop song I remember from my Alexandria days, her new shoes pounding the dust only slightly behind us.

When we reach the shadowed ravine between the bluffs,

we stare up the cliff sides. Then we're zigzagging from one wall to the other, jumping between boulders and sliding along slippery patches as we laugh, clap, and roll like an artistic troupe that has been performing together for years.

At the base of the maple tree, we pause reverently and U-turn around it, Karam and me joining hands and briefly touching lips. Then I lead a dash back down the ravine floor to the sagging pier on the river and dare everyone to stand on it, looking into the water.

"But won't it collapse under all our weight?" Pearl asks nervously.

"Have faith," I tease her.

She giggles and moves bravely to join the crowd.

Our wrinkled reflections peer up at us, rippled by the breeze. The others may see the Richland parkour club, but I also see dimpled Jaleela and the rest of Karam's family, smiling wide, wishing us well, hands raised with ours.

"Be strong to be useful," I recite.

"*Etre fort pour être utile,*" everyone responds.

ACKNOWLEDGMENTS

Above all, I (Pam) wish to acknowledge my co-author Arooj Hayat, who was fun and inspirational to work with.

Also, enormous appreciation for Alyssa Serpa: parkour athlete, coach, and manager of Origins Parkour and Athletic Facility in Vancouver, Canada.
Check her out on you tube at:

- Alyssa Serpa - Ongoing Thing / 2014 (Origins Parkour)
- Alyssa Serpa's 2017 Redbull Art of Motion Submission
- The ParkourEDU Podcast Ep. 16 — Alyssa Serpa
- Alyssa Serpa / YEAR 7
- Alyssa Serpa / Year 8

Imam Shujaath Ali of Vancouver also was kind enough to meet with me.

I appreciate the input of Gail Murphy, professor in the Department of Computer Science and associate vice president of research at the University of British Columbia, as well as co-founder and chief scientist at Tasktop Technologies Inc. And her son, Jason Murphy.

I owe a debt of gratitude to my son Jeremy Withers, my husband Steve Withers, Allyson Latta, Scott Fraser, and my agents Lynn Bennett and Amy Tomkins. Also Shahira Clemens, Vansh Bali, Anita Lau, Bella Nelstrop, Silvana Bevilacqua, and Lindsay Vine. And my sister Priscilla Fox.

Also, the (mostly Muslim) students in Anita Lau's class who offered feedback: Melody, Laura, Zuha, Rania, Jabriil ("the book doesn't make all Muslims into terrorists like a lot of stuff does"), Nayis, Carter, Alex, Andrea, and Daniel.

I (Arooj) would like to acknowledge Pam Withers for giving me this opportunity to showcase Muslim thinking and culture in a fun book for young adults. It was an honour to be able to work with her on this project.

I also want to acknowledge the countless young Muslims in Canada who are always striving for excellence – be it academics, sports, leadership, research, poetry, business – and setting examples in their communities. I am inspired by all of you. And so I dedicate this book to you, the young Muslims, who know the struggle of living as a "visible Muslim" in this society. I know how hard it is growing up with your feet in two worlds, striving to strike a balance, and always having to act like an ambassador for your religion and your culture. And yet, you all keep doing good, smiling, and winning at whatever you choose to take on. Keep it up!

Last but not least, I wish to dedicate this book to my little daughter, my nieces and nephews, and ALL the children of their generation, growing up in a scary world. May Allah always protect you, strengthen you with moral clarity, conviction, faith, and patience, and make you a shining beacon of hope for a better future, Ameen.

This book was inspired partly by four films of Aden Freerunners:

- *Fearless Freerunners*
- *Rise*
- *Loud*
- *Somewhere*

Books we found helpful:

- *Crossing the Sea with Syrians on the Exodus to Europe* by Wolfgang Bauer (andotherstories.org, 2016)
- *I Am Nujoo, Age Ten and Divorced,* by Nujood Ali and Delphine Minoui
- *In the Skin of a Jihadist: A Young Journalist Enters the ISIS Recruitment Network* by Anna Erelle
- *Intolerable: A Memoir of Extremes* by Kamal Al-Solaylee
- *Radicalized* by Alexander Dhand
- *Radicalized: New Jihadists and the Threat to the West* by Peter R. Neumann
- *The Way of the Strangers: Encounters with the Islamic State* by Graeme Wood

Documentary:

- *CBC: Undercover in ISIS*

Articles:

- "Answers to Frequently Asked Questions about Muslims"
- "Nine Questions About ISIS You Were Too Embarrassed to Ask"

ABOUT THE AUTHORS

Pam Withers is the award-winning author of twenty-one young-adult novels, including *Andreo's Race, Tracker's Canyon,* and *Stowaway.* She lives in Vancouver, Canada. Her website is www.pamwithers.com.

Arooj Hayat immigrated to Canada as a child (eleven years old). A Doctor of Pharmacy student, health blogger, fitness coach, mom, and former youth leader of her masjid (mosque), she lives in Richmond, British Columbia, Canada.

THE INSIDE STORY OF WRITING THE PARKOUR CLUB BY PAM WITHERS

This novel was originally inspired by volunteer work I did with Syrian refugees the summer of 2016. My reasoning was simple and naive: Feature a refugee boy trying to adapt to life in an American high school. (We ended up making him a secondary character, and his Caucasian love-interest the main character.)

I knew the lens would be through a parkour club, because a number of readers had been asking me to feature the sport of parkour, a combination of jujitsu, gymnastics and running that enjoys worldwide participation. It's very popular among youth!

Little did I know what dark twists and turns the seed of the plot would take me from there.

First, I began searching for websites of parkour clubs in the Middle East. I settled on having a protagonist from Yemen when I came across four highly inspiring films of Aden Freerunners in Yemen:

- *Fearless Freerunners*
- *Rise*
- *Loud*
- *Somewhere*

Next, casting about for an antagonist, I uneasily knew I had one after reading *In the Skin of a Jihadist: A Young Journalist Enters the ISIS Recruitment Network* by Anna Erelle. Yes, recruiters target teens and young people, and it was spookily easy to find their recruiting criteria, literature and much else on the internet.

Of course, long before I started outlining or writing, I knew I needed to work with an understanding person from the Muslim community. The BC Muslim Association hooked me up with Arooj Hayat, then a youth leader for her mosque in Burnaby, British Columbia, Canada. We connected immediately, both being extroverts, and had laughs and hugs from the very first session in a coffee shop. I invited Arooj to become my co-author, and she helped write dialogue and brainstorm plot twists, while also ensuring the terminology in the novel was respectful of her faith.

She answered all my questions with true openness, patience, grace and the occasional giggle. Happily for me, she seemed to get a kick out of everything from "decorating" our character Pearl's room, to supplying Arabic words. Truth be told, Pearl is modeled somewhat after Arooj, and of course Pearl ended up playing a much bigger part in the novel than we previously planned.

When it came time to get a photograph of ourselves as co-authors, Arooj was reluctant to do it because she'd just gotten married, and then pregnant! But what fun we had the day she finally put her toddler in childcare and came to a photographer's studio to pair up for goofing around in front of the camera.

Also through the BC Muslim Association, I met Imam Shujaath Ali of Vancouver, who was kind enough to answer some challenging questions, later discussed with Arooj.

Meanwhile, **Alyssa Serpa** – parkour athlete, coach and manager of Origins Parkour and Athletic Facility in Vancouver, Canada – spent hours helping with plot points and parkour move descriptions. She "choreographed" the parkour scenes, especially the climax chase, after being given a framework to work within. What a gift to have her on board!

Of course, the plot would never have worked without some knowledge of how our characters were using and manipulating the internet. That's where Gail Murphy came in. Despite her super-busy life as professor in the Department of Computer Science at the University of British Columbia, vice president of research at UBC, and co-founder and chief scientist at Tasktop Technologies Inc., she brainstormed that plot aspect, and also involved her teen son, Jason Murphy.

Apologies to residents of Richland, Washington, USA for messing with your geography a little :). Yes, you have a mosque, and a butte that is well above the river. Yes, you have red maple trees. No, that butte doesn't have a ravine that divides it into twin buttes, and we even had the nerve to make up a high school name. That's called creative license.

Special thanks to editor Allyson Latta, and to our photographer, Larry Scherben of Camera One Photography.

Anita Lau, a teacher of pre-teens in Richmond, B.C.,

Canada offered to read the manuscript to a group in her school, a reading club with many recent immigrants, some Muslim. She generously shared their feedback with us:

Anita: "Excited to say we started reading your manuscript today. Got permission from the principal and sent home a note to parents. R snuggles right beside me when I read and is very attached to every word. Being a recent immigrant, she really 'gets' the story on an emotional level. Today, she broke into tears as she shared how she had to leave a favorite auntie behind. Z and R nod in consensus to the parts about how it's important to be modest in dress. R shared with us that it's her dad who decides what she can and cannot wear (skirts, shorts not allowed yet)."

Students:

J: Doesn't make all Muslims into terrorists like a lot of stuff does.

C: Felt like Karam, the main character, is sitting in the circle with us and telling the story.

D: Makes me want to learn more parkour.

A: Very shady and mysterious.

J: In our religion, the hijab is the girl's crown. In [my town], at the halal store, people stare at my mom if she's not covered up, but Mom ignores them. But she wants to wear her hijab to pray in the mosque.

R: (just immigrated to Canada) It was hard to leave my home country, my friends and family. We are lucky to be the few who were chosen to come to Canada. In Canada, I felt better when I met Z and her family because they are from the same place. I felt connected to my culture. We left with four boxes. We had to give up our beautiful home and all the furniture and luxuries.

Z: My mom cried so hard when we had to leave. I was very sad. Social media helps our family keep in touch with people back home.

J: My dad was shot in the leg in Somalia. When he left, there were lots of dangers like pirates in the international waters. But he made it to Canada.

C: My dad and his family had to flee Vietnam and get to international waters. It was dangerous. The government helped the refugees. The boats were 25 meters long and 5 meters wide, packed with 500 people. Lots of people drowned.

J: I felt the tension and the suspense.

L: I can feel the darkness.

R: Did an imam help you with the religious parts? Why did this you choose Islam as the religion for your book?

J: The kids at [Richland] high school are ignorant about Muslims and it really irritates me, being Muslim.

L: [re Richland High girl scenes]: Fun to read; in real life, girls are like that.

And then, the teacher arranged for these students to visit Alyssa's parkour studio, meet her and me, and try out the sport. (A *very* popular field trip.)

Another friend of mine, a person of colour and Muslim upbringing who immigrated to England, and then Canada as a child, also read the manuscript and offered me this feedback...

Shahira: Your book is one of the few places anyone has questioned why parents with young children would go to such great lengths to flee a country in which their family has lived for generations, if they were terrorists themselves.

Karam seemed to be welcomed into the Richland High school community quickly and without much resistance. In my experience, there are only one or two students who extend the hand of friendship, while others remain suspicious for some time. It's tough to be accepted when you're a different colour, even when you speak English well and don't come from a Muslim country. Teenagers tend to regurgitate what's being said around their dinner table about immigrants, and most of it is negative. I like your optimism that Pearl and Karam's Islamic info session is so well attended. Maybe I'm too cynical, but I would expect very few attendees the first time. Or if many came, I would expect their questions to be more antagonistic.

Pam again: When I got stuck on a plot point one wintery day while visiting my son (a graduate student in Toronto), I asked him if he would brainstorm with me for a few minutes. Jeremy has traveled widely in the Middle East (including Jordan, Israel, Syria, Egypt and Morocco), and we ended up working on the story together for almost two hours. What a generous gift of time and knowledge-sharing that was!

Arooj and I continue to stay in touch (I just sewed her daughter a quilt), and we both hope the book will inspire cross-cultural, cross-religious insight and tolerance. I would like to end by reprinting Arooj's book dedication.

Arooj Hayat: I dedicate this book to you, the young Muslims, who know the struggle of living as a "visible Muslim" in this society. I know how hard it is growing up with your feet in two worlds, striving to strike a balance, and always having to act like an ambassador for your religion and your culture. And yet, you all keep doing good, smiling, and winning at whatever you choose to take on. Keep it up!

I also wish to dedicate this book to my little daughter, my nieces and nephews, and ALL the children of their generation, growing up in a scary world. May Allah always protect you, strengthen you with moral clarity, conviction, faith, and patience, and make you a shining beacon of hope for a better future, Ameen.

CPSIA information can be obtained
at www.ICGtesting.com
Printed in the USA
LVHW021657200521
688018LV00010B/1037

9 780995 910324